Paula Green lives on Auckland's west coast with her partner, artist Michael Hight, their two daughters, three cats and two springer spaniels. A poet, reviewer, anthologist, blogger and children's author, she has published ten poetry collections including several for children. Her latest collection is *The Letterbox Cat and Other Poems*.

Paula regularly visits schools through the New Zealand Book Council and privately. She runs NZ Poetry Box nzwordpoetrybox.wordpress.com, an interactive blog for children, teachers and parents from Year 0 to Year 8. When she is not writing, she loves walking, running, biking, swimming, boogie-boarding, reading, cooking, watching movies, listening to music and visiting new places.

In 2017 she won the Prime Minister's Award for Poetry and was admitted to the New Zealand Order of Merit for Services to Literature and Poetry.

a treasury of NZ poems for children

For my mother, Margaret Green – PG
For Kenese and Kalia – Mum

RANDOM HOUSE

UK | USA | Canada | Ireland | Australia
India | New Zealand | South Africa | China

Random House is an imprint of the Penguin Random House group of companies,
whose addresses can be found at global.penguinrandomhouse.com.

Penguin
Random House
New Zealand

First published by Random House New Zealand, 2014
This edition published by Penguin Random House New Zealand, 2017

10 9 8 7 6 5 4 3 2 1

Selection and introduction © Paula Green, 2014
Illustrations © Jenny Cooper, 2014
© in individual poems remains with the authors

Design by Megan van Staden © Penguin Random House New Zealand
Prepress by Image Centre Group
Printed and bound in China by RR Donnelley Asia Printing Solutions Ltd

A catalogue record for this book is available from the National Library of New Zealand.

ISBN 978-0-14377-219-4

penguin.co.nz

a treasury of NZ poems for children

Edited by Paula Green
Illustrated by Jenny Cooper

RANDOM HOUSE
NEW ZEALAND

Introduction

Poetry

When you unwrap a poem you might find
sizzling butter in the pancake pan

the flight of a kite in the deep blue sky
crackling laughter when you all say cheese

the look of love in your grandmother's eye
words that taste sweet and words that hop

doorways and windows and rickety gates
tickets to space and a wild west wind

This poetry anthology is like a treasure box in which you can go digging and delving for gold and silver, cups and mugs and precious stones. You will find poems that shine, poems that sing and poems that whisper. Some poems tell stories and some poems act the goat. There are poems about cats, cows and elephants, the sun, the sea and the stars.

Some of the poems were written a very long time ago (James K Baxter, Eileen Duggan, Denis Glover), while some poets and poems are very new (Elena de Roo, Stephanie Mayne). You will discover poems by some of our most beloved children's authors (Gavin Bishop,

Joy Cowley, David Hill, Margaret Mahy, Kyle Mewburn) and poems by some of our most beloved adult writers (Jenny Bornholdt, Fiona Farrell, Sam Hunt, Michele Leggott, Bill Manhire, Elizabeth Smither, Brian Turner, Hone Tuwhare).

Some of these poems were first published in *The School Journal* (I loved falling upon a poem when I read the journals as a child!), while other poems have never been published before. Some poems (such as Peter Bland's) have already appeared in gorgeous books of their own (another poetry hunt for you!).

When you go hunting you will find poems written by poets when they were very young (Sam Hunt, Katherine Mansfield, Laura Ranger, Gloria Rawlinson). You will also find the twenty winners of A Fabulous Poetry Competition for Children. Nearly two thousand poems were sent to me from Cape Reinga to Bluff and my study was a glittering palace of words.

Looking in the treasure box will be like travelling through night and day, night and day, night and day. You might discover a poem that makes you laugh, a poem that makes you sad, a poem that makes you think, and a poem that makes you wriggle right out of your skin!

Pick a poem from the treasure box, hold it up to the light, find your favourite, cosy spot and start reading. Or, even better, pick a poem, hold it up to the light, find your favourite, cosy reading spot and then get someone else to read it to you.

Paula Green

Words

Some words just feel nice
like green apple butter
and blue lemon ice
or soft mossy pillows
by whispering willows
and tamarind trees
in a hot summer breeze

they sing on your tongue
no reason to be
some words just hum
like the cat on your knee

Elena de Roo

Buzz

Early

The darkness wears a quiet sound
of fires died down and people who stir
in sleep. Soon they will slip on
their daily selves, button them up.

A rooster knows the time, says
it out loud when day is less
than a light line above the hills.

A car hitches its shoulders,
decides to keep going.
Its lights make holes in the night.

One ruru calls
its own name.
Its wings are invisible.
They make no sound.

Rachel Bush

The Poet

As the clouds change in the wind,
As the world spins slowly,
As birds fly over the treetops,
And dogs bark in the distance . . .

I write this poem in my hammock.

Caleb James Apiata Stewart of Ngāpuhi, aged 12

Girl Reading

She overhears the sound of things in hiding.
She bites an apple and imagines orchard starlight.
Each time she licks her thumb, its tip,
she tastes the icy branches,
she hears a sigh migrate from page to page.

Bill Manhire

Autumn Leaves

Red leaves
gold leaves
get as loose
as my front teeth
then they fall out.

In granny's garden
the tall oak tree
is as old as my mother.
It makes a red leaf carpet
on the ground.

Swish swish
I make a wish.
Lie on the magic carpet,
fly to the gold palace.
Swim in the
sea of leaves.
Swish swish swish
as quiet as a fish.

Laura Ranger, written when she was 6

A Visit to the Beachside Library

I'd rather be lost
in a sea of words
than in an ocean of water.

Bill Nagelkerke

The Big Black Whale

I wish I were a big, black whale
Out in the deep green sea.
He blows like a hose
Through the top of his nose,
As happy as a whale can be,
And the sailors look pale
When they hear his tail
Go smack, smack, smack,
On a big wave's back
Out in the deep green sea.

James K Baxter

Tree Cat

Bird in a tree,
Sleep, sleep, sleep.
Cat climbed up,
Steep, stecp, steep.
Bird opened eye,
Peep, peep, peep.
Cat about to
Leap, leap, leap.
Bird flew away,
Cheep, cheep, cheep.
Cat slunk home,
Creep, creep, creep.

Joy Cowley

Our Dog Charlie

Our dog Charlie
is such a softie that
sparrows eat their
breakfast
perched upon his
back.

No one's scared of
Charlie.
He smiles when
he's asleep
dreaming of days in
the country
being rounded up
by sheep.

Peter Bland

Bumbles

Nothing pleases the big
bumble bees

busy and bee-loud
in the tree

outside my kitchen window
more than the

yellow flowers
that they snuggle

up to and joggle,
dithering

and humming
happily.

Brian Turner

The Bumble-bee Postie

From letterbox to letterbox
the postie flits,
dropping our letters
and cards through the slits;
on grey days and blue days,
in sunshine and showers —
like a bicycling bumble-bee
sipping the flowers.

John Parker

My Cat

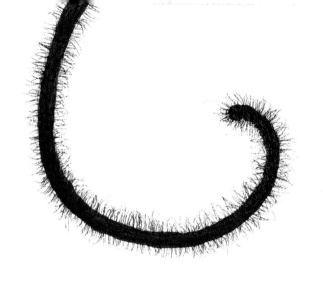

He scratches like a hen
And growls like a dog.
He hisses like a snake.
He jumps like a frog.
He creeps like a lizard.
He climbs like a goat.
And he purrs like the motor
Of a fishing boat.

He mews like a gull.
He runs like a hare.
He pounces like a lion.
He eats like a bear.
He plays like a monkey.
He walks like a duck.
And he purrs like the engine
Of the milkman's truck.

Joy Cowley

Statue Cat

She sits there watching me
Her ears are snow-capped
Her black tail coils around her
She has a perfectly shaped pink nose
Her little white paws
Line up four in a row
Her rough pink tongue sticks out
I would like her better if she wasn't wooden

Eden Matthews, aged 10

Cocoon

At night,
when it's cold and frosty,
I wriggle-wiggle into my sleeping bag
and curl up tight,
like a caterpillar in a cocoon
that's just been spun.

And soon
I'm so warm and snug
I could sleep for months,
then wake in the spring
as a butterfly
to stretch my wings in the sun.

John Parker

Getting a Fish

I found him in a fish tank
I said to my mum and dad, 'Can I have him?'
He is the size of a bee

Lachlan Boniface, aged 7

23

Sun Sonata

The sun shone a tree
over my yard today;
stretched its
long black arms
around my garden
and into my house
where thin
dark fingers
played a small masterpiece
on my arm.

Elizabeth Pulford

Weather Forecast

The magician at the weather office
Is stirring a pot of clouds
And wind around.

No cyclone today, Mr Magician.
No, he says. Today there will be
Fine spells.

Janice Marriott

Thunder God

Over the dark sky I gather
lightning lives within me
the clouds are my cloak
hear my pain see my anger feel my power
beware
I am the thunder god

Apirana Taylor

The Orchard

It is all calm until the wind starts to moan like
a dog howling in pain,
leaves are rustling like tin foil getting stood on,
the trees are as big as a dinosaur flapping
its wings,
in the orchard.

Adam Scammell, aged 10

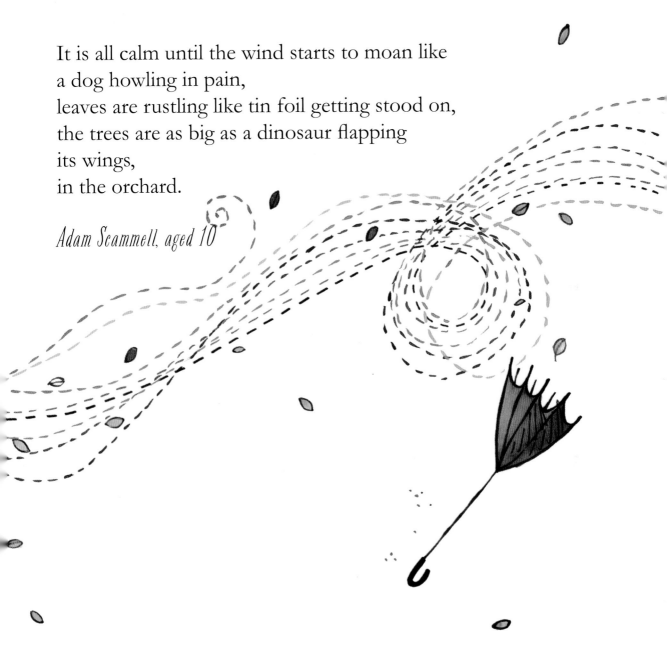

Little Mr Mushroom

Little Mr Mushroom
Underneath a tree,
I look at you
And you look at me.

You grow from the grass
In a single night
With your round, round hat
And your head so white.

You have no hands
Or feet to run;
You stand and blink
At the morning sun.

Little Mr Mushroom,
What would I do
If you were I
And I were you?

James K Baxter

Tulip Sunday

In the Botanical Gardens
bright tulips
spread out
like a yellow tablecloth
on a table with thousands of legs.

Some tulips
have red lips
and dark black eyes.
They bow and curtsy
in the wind.

Laura Ranger, written when she was 6

The Bookshop Elephant

An elephant lives in our bookshop,
beside the paperback shelf.
Any time of the day you will see her,
reading silently to herself.

If you try to interrupt her,
she'll raise her large grey trunk,
flap her large grey ears and go:
Booketty, booketty, hump!

She reads adventure and mystery
but what she likes the most
is a very scary yarn about
a haunted house and a ghost.

If you yell, 'Boo!' behind her,
she'll raise her large grey trunk,
flap her large grey ears and go:
Booketty, booketty, jump!

Boo

She's read a whole section on ballet,
and she thinks she knows how to dance.
She's even bought a pink tutu
should someone give her a chance.

If you ask her to dance for you,
she'll raise her large grey trunk,
flap her large grey ears and go:
Booketty, booketty, bump!

She's studied from Ants to Zebras.
She knows the history of art.
Give her a look at a poetry book
and she learns all the rhymes by heart.

If she's asked to leave the shop,
she'll raise her large grey trunk,
flap her large grey ears and go:
Booketty, booketty, grump!

Joy Cowley

Hippopotamus

Watery, snortery potamus thing
Asleep in your bath full of mud
You never have to get out of the water
And go off to school like the rest of us ought'a
Do you ever think what tomorrow will bring?
Lumbery, slumbery potamus thing

Nosy old, dozy old potamus thing
Surrounded by water and lilies
You look a lot like an old submarine
That's got sort of tired, and run out of steam
I'll bet you never get out for a fling
Stayabout, layabout potamus thing

Corny old, yawny old potamus thing
Do the lily pads tickle your nose?
Most people wash every night before bed
But you have a bath to get dirty instead
Stuck in the mud like a lazy old king
Lubberly, bubbly potamus thing

Crinkly old, wrinkly old potamus thing
You've got a good place in the water
Pitamus, potamus, sleepy it seems
Just dreaming those tired hippopotamus dreams
Even your name has a slow sort of ring
Wallowy, swallowy, potamus thing.

Jon Gadsby

The Armadillo

You would not choose to use
An armadillo
For a pillow.
Its armoured scales
Are hard as nails
And lumpy.
You'd wake up grumpy.
Nor would you care to share
Its favourite luncheon
Of ants to munch on.

Shirley Gawith

Once a Little Kiwifruit

Once a little kiwifruit, just for fun,
took off his jacket and lay in the sun.
'Be careful, dear,' his mother said.
'Or you'll burn a nasty red.
It's not wise for a kiwifruit
to sunbathe in his birthday suit.'
BUT . . .
He lay there on his rug and pillow,
and woke up as a tamarillo.

Fiona Farrell

35

Big Birds and Small

Big birds and small
Surround a slice of bread
Spread with butter.

The small birds come first
Quickly, boldly
They peck like a sewing machine

Sewing tiny stitches.
The big birds swagger
Full of importance

They bite the bread
Into buttonholes.
Then big birds and small

Tear it all to pieces.

Elizabeth Smither

Driving Through the Apple Orchards

Like golden moons
the apples freeze
upon the frosty winter trees
with nobody
to feel or care
how lonely they look
        hanging there.

I think
how lovely it would be
if some of them belonged
                to me.

Peggy Dunstan

Tuatara

The old survivor, tuatara,
reptilian great-grandfather,
observing with heavy-lidded eye
the still old centuries passing by,

slow little bloke in enamel coat
shedding his tail, croaking his croak,
his third eye watching world upon world,
an eternity to have, to hold.

Lauris Edmond

The Growly Bear

The growly bear,
The growly bear,
He lives in the cupboard
Under the stair.

His hat and his boots
And his breeches are brown,
And he sleeps all day
On a brown eiderdown.

At night he goes walking
About by himself
To gobble up the honey
On the kitchen shelf.

You can hear him growling
Wherever he goes,
But just what he looks like
Nobody knows.

James K Baxter

Sunflowers

Dad thinks
they look like clowns.
Mum says
they're overgrown
    daisies.

Either way
there's always a buzz
when they raise their
    heads
and sway in the sun.

Bees love them.
So do I.

Peter Bland

The Daisy

Each day the daisy
Opens its face
Like a plate.
The sky washes it
With cloud suds
And clear blue water.
Now it is clean.
At the centre of the plate
Is a tiny egg for dinner.

Elizabeth Smither

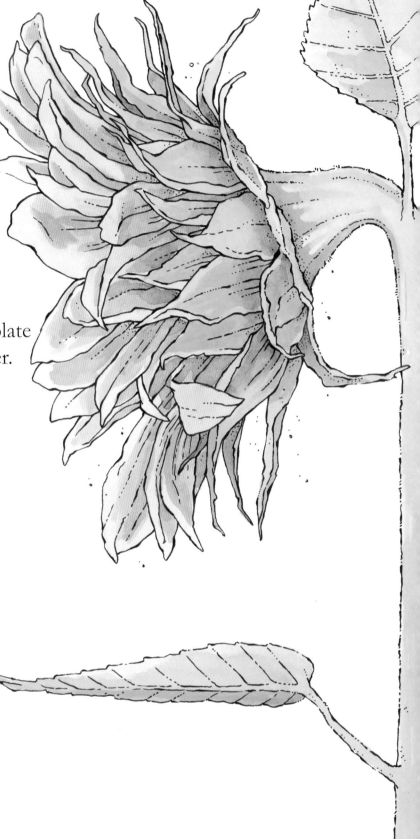

Pekapeka

You see the world
in sounds you sing,

in echoes that sing
back to you

of all that's out there
solid through.

You sing to see
and sing to love,

fighting for a singing post
to win the one you love the most

by singing how
the world should be.

Your hands are wings,
your eyes are song.

Pekapeka,
sing on.

Anna Jackson

Ode to the Orange

for Christopher

You hoard up sweetness
through the long hot days,
through the slow autumn burn,
and when winter comes
you are plump and full of smiles.
You bring your crescents
of sun to all our winter soccer
games, our mouths crowded
with peel, our cold fingers
sticky with summer.
We can peel you
in one long snake of fire,
or squeeze you, your golden heart
spilling into our cold glasses.
Always fair, you let yourself
be divided up, each precious
bag of juice neatly packed
for travel. Fat orange friend
from the warm north,
I will throw you up high
in the sky, you will be my sun
through the dark winter days
and your sweet juice
will keep me well
till summer returns.

Sarah Broom

It Is Nearly Summer

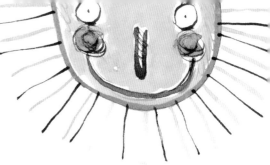

A rubber duck is paddling up the sky.
The world is a constant amazement,
always on the move.
It is nearly summer. It is nearly autumn.

Bill Manhire

Shiny

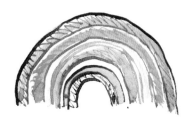

It's a bright shiny world
as it's meant to be.
Clear shiny rivers
and wide shiny sea.
Bright shiny flowers,
happy birds,
buzzy bees.
Bright shiny world,
happy you,
happy me.

Fiona Farrell

Earth

How does the earth do it

how are we

not falling down?

Dinah Hawken

Estuary Dance

Pied oystercatchers pirouette across the field
ballerinas in an overgrown lawn.

Hip-hop herons breakdance in the estuary
speckles of mud splash in the water.

Crabs scuttle and waltz into the unknown
underground karaoke bars.

Children skim stones and the ripples
dance across the river mouth.

Holly Guthrie, aged 12

Bright 1

Temuera says the sun
looks like a piece
of kauri gum

Robert Sullivan

Mum

Her hair curls
like fern fronds.

Her eyes are like
speckled green birds' eggs.

Her glasses are two pools
of clear water.

Her nose is blunt.

Her hands are wrinkled and kind.
She reaches out to touch me.

I love my mum
forty four million
times around the world.

Laura Ranger, written when she was 7

Rainy Day Washaway

Glum, drab and gloomy, dribbly and grey,
it looked like rain . . . again.
If Evie was stuck in the house one more day
she'd be bored right out of her brain!

Then all of a sudden, a brainwave struck!
(From where, she wasn't certain.)
If the sky was a window, with any luck,
the clouds were like dirty curtains.

So Evie rang Sophie, then Sophie rang Shay,
and together they hatched a plan.
'Why don't we just wash all this weather away?'
'If anyone can, we can!'

They fetched a big wash-tub, a ladder and net,
then tied some pegs to a rope.
As the tub filled with water, so hot and so wet,
they squirted in super-suds soap.

Then Evie and Sophie climbed up to the sky,
and clipped each peg to a cloud.
They leapt into space as though they could fly
and bungeed back down to the ground.

With a HEAVE! and a HO! they hauled the clouds under
and squished them into the tub.
They crackled with lightning and rumbled with thunder
as they all got a jolly good scrub.

They hung all the clouds in orderly rows,
from small to middle to big.
Then wound up the hoist as high as it goes,
till it span like a whirligig.

Shay pointed his hose at the cloud-stained sun
and turned the tap on full blast.
It sizzled and steamed but when it was done,
it dried again really fast.

Up they all hopped with their buckets and mops
and rags all tied in a bunch.
But what did they do when they reached the top?
They sat down and ate their lunch.

They wiped away sunspots and meteor streaks
and melted moon cheese like glue.
Then they scrubbed the sky until it squeaked,
so clear you could see right through.

As they wound down the hoist a cloud got snagged
on the man-in-the-moon's pointy chin.
They sewed it together with fine silver thread
and a shiny gold safety-pin.

By now all the clouds were lovely and dry,
fluffy and light as a feather.
Evie cheered as they floated back up to the sky,
'That looks like much better weather.'

Out of their houses the children all poured,
shouting, 'Hip Hip Hooray!'
Surely Evie couldn't be bored
with such a glorious day?

But cleaning the sky had been so much fun
Evie had a brainwave . . . again!
One day soon when they'd had enough sun
they could try to make it rain.

Kyle Mewburn

The Albadile and the Crocotross

Did you know the albadile has lost her smile?
She sneaks down to the water on crocodile feet

but hunts for fish with an albatross beak.
The crocotross is equally cross.

He soars through the air with spectacular wings
that spread like ferns on his albatross back,

but his jaw full of teeth is itching to swing
on some tasty bones to crack and snap!

Paula Green

Birthday Cake Recipe

Crush a pound of Crocketts
In a Cricketty crack

Cream some Wordle Wober
And the Whippersnap

Mix some crackers with Dordle Dackers
And lots of Lumper lollies

Now bake on low and don't let go
Then cool down caper among the vapour

Time to ice your Sprinkering Tack
Shake on slime crinkled bats

Crackle spiddle pop spatt

Oh sweet Whippersnap!

Sarah Aileen

Computers Can't Scoot

My rich old Uncle Fred
wants to buy me a gift, he said.
'I will get you a scooter
or a brand new computer,
but you can't have both,' he said.

Tomorrow he's going away
so I have to decide today.
But computers can't scoot
and a scooter can't compute —
so what am I going to say?

Rachel McAlpine

My Sister

My sister's remarkably light,
She can float to a fabulous height.
It's a troublesome thing,
But we tie her with string,
And we use her instead of a kite.

Margaret Mahy

Big Blue Mouth

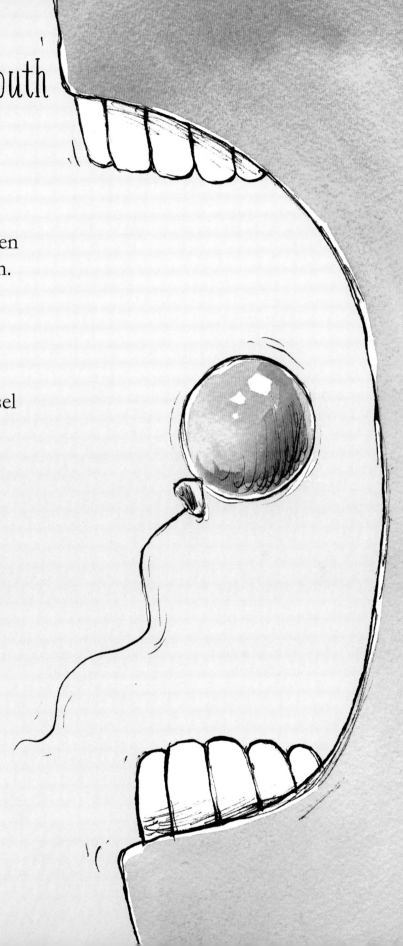

The sky is a
big blue mouth.

Already it has eaten
the daylight moon.

What next?
The sun?

No. A mere morsel
will do.

It opens wide
and swallows

my yellow
runaway balloon.

John Malone

Shearing Shed

The first ewe up —
bleat, bleat,
flailing feet;
zing-zing
near her ear.
Shears cut a mossy track.
Wool curls like soft butter
and spills across greasy floors.

The last sweep.
The fleece,
like a dropped overcoat,
is gathered in wide shiny arms,
packed,
and weighed.

The last ewe totters,
chatters,
tap-dances down the ramp
and leaps free —
naked,
blushing,
as pink as a prawn.

Wendy Clarke

Cows in Drought

The cows are sad.
They've eaten all the grass.
There's only one shady tree to share.
One trough that I sit in,
one hot sun beating down,
one gazillion flies
and no rain in sight.

Emily Boulton, aged 10

Country Roast

The rocky road curves
like a potato peel.

Gravel crunches
pork crackling
under car wheels.

The smell of the sheep
is burnt baking
just out of the oven.

Grass surrounds the house
a pool of gravy.

Alexandra Swain, aged 12

Palomino

I like it when

                  the wind climbs

sunburned hills

              and the grass shivers

like the hairs

                on a pony's back

and a toetoe mane

             flows over my shoulder

as we gallop

          and gallop

               and gallop away

Vivienne Joseph

61

Zoo Chimpanzee

Visitor, what do you see
When you behold a chimpanzee?
You point, you stare, you gasp, you gape
It's hard to tell who is the ape.
If we share a family tree
You can't climb it quick as me.
You eat meat, which must taste vile
I prefer food veggie style.
Your hands are weak, useless paws
It's faster running on all fours.
You daft humans make me laugh
You go to school. You take a bath!
Frankly it is hard to see
Who is caged and who is free!
I play with food, I scratch, I bite
I misbehave, I shove, I fight
If folk do not like my chatter
Hey — what they think doesn't matter
When I tire of a crowd
I whoop a bit and screech out loud
Then turn around and bare my bum
I bet you've never had such fun!

Stephanie Mayne

George's Pet

When George and his gorilla
Go bounding down the street,
They get respectful nods and smiles
From neighbours that they meet.

If George had owned a puppy dog,
Or else a kitty-cat,
His neighbours wouldn't notice him
With courtesy like that.

Margaret Mahy

bow-wow! bow-wow! bow-wow! bow-wow!

Four Bow-wow Poems

The First Bow-wow Poem

You woke my mother up this morning
At six o'clock with your barking

So she took away your barks
And put them in the bow-wow box

She tied you up and took your barks away
Now all you do is smile at strangers all day

You aren't a guard dog any more
You aren't even a dog any more!

The Second Bow-wow Poem

I don't really think that I like
A dog that can't bark when he likes

So all by myself this afternoon
I took the bow-wow box down

It was hidden in behind a lot of books
And I gave you back eleven big barks

bow-wow! bow-wow bow-wow! bow-wow bow-wow bow-wow bow-wow bow-wow! bow-wow! bow-wow!

You've run outside to use them up
I think you've woken the baby up!

The Third Bow-wow Poem

Look, here are some simple facts:
You'll find in the poetry books
One-thousand-and-twelve poems about cats

There are all sorts of poems about cats
Some chasing rats and others wearing hats
And poems about cats that simply sit on mats

But you look for bow-wow poetry
And it's quite a different story:
Right now there are only three.

And One Makes Four

They often ask me why
I write this bow-wow poetry

I'll tell you
And cross-my-heart it's true

I've got nothing else to do.

Sam Hunt

Winter Fly

A slow winter fly
ambles across the rug.

The cat watches
idly
curiously
intently
maliciously
Wham!

The fly just manages it.
A low, bumbling
zooming flight
in the nick of time.

Adrienne Jansen

Scratchy Cats

I don't like scratchy cats at all,
They tear the paper on the wall,
And swing on curtains pulling threads,
And claw the covers on the beds.
They scratch up plants, which makes my dad
Who's put them in get really mad.
Their sharp claws scratch the furniture,
Indeed, there seems to be no cure
For scratchy cats, but their worst sin
Is when they pounce and scratch my skin.

Shirley Gawith

67

The Elephant Bird

The elephant is a remarkable bird.
Her wings look like ears and her tail is absurd.
She has no real beak, but instead has a nose
that goes on and on, like a fat rubber hose.

She doesn't lay eggs, and she's no good at flying.
(I really believe she has given up trying!)
Another strange thing . . . she has four legs, not two,
and she nests on the ground, in the jungle or zoo.

She doesn't sing well. The last one I heard
sounded more like a train or a bull than a bird!
Her feathers aren't soft, they are bristly and grey,
and when she comes round, other birds fly away.

She's a bit too heavy to perch in a tree
and she doesn't look terribly bird-like to me,
so I'll start this poem again if you wish . . .
'The elephant is a remarkable fish . . .'

Joy Watson

An Elephanty Poem

Loom large
Jumbo diddy elephiddy
Large loom
Jambo daddy elephaddy
Looming barge
Jimbo doddy elephinty
Large boom
Jumbo body elephanty

Paula Green

The Ships

The little ships
From the harbour sail
Bang in the teeth
Of a southerly gale.

The great white waves
Wash to and fro:
Drum, drum, drum,
Say the engines below.

With their oilskins on
The captains stand;
They drop their nets
Far out from land.

And they bring home,
For you and me,
Snapper and groper
And terakihi.

Then the little ships
At anchor lie,
And the captains' coats
Hang up to dry.

James K Baxter

The Bed Boat

My bed is a boat.
The mattress won't leak.
My head-board's a rudder,
my sail is a sheet.

I sail every night
exploring my room,
past wardrobes like ships,
past mirrors like moons.

As I drift into sleep
my bed-boat sails on,
though where it sails to
is known to no one.

But when I wake up,
my voyage safely done,
I throw back the curtains
and let in the sun.

Peter Bland

The Red Pencil Sharpener

I am looking down the barrels of
the red pencil sharpener,
its holes
big as drainpipes,
fat as full moons,
flared like the nostrils
of horses.

They are
deep wells,
dark tunnels,
O-shaped mouths hungry
for pencils.

The red pencil sharpener sharpens
my imagination.

John Malone

The Lid Slides Back

Let me open
my pencil-case made of native woods.
It is light and dark in bits and pieces.
The lid slides back.

The seven pencils are there, called *Lakeland*.
I could draw a sunset.
I could draw the stars.
I could draw this quiet tree beside the water.

Bill Manhire

It's More Simple for Dogs

I put on my boots
My overtrousers
My jacket
My hat
My scarf
Gloves.

I put on my dog's
Collar and lead.

We're both ready
For anything.

Janice Marriott

Jimbo

We've lost Jimbo. Her hollow on the couch
is cold. We've crawled through every gap, checked

every door, but now, at dusk, the sky is coming down
and she's not home. Some bird-rustle, tree-shimmy, rat-scent

has taken her. We prowl the neighbourhood,
searching, not with our eyes, but with our instincts,

sensing how the dark is poised to pounce. Shadows
ripple like pelts. Lamp posts arch; cars growl;

roses flex their claws. The sharp teeth of stars
begin to gleam. Hope trembles, then curls into a ball.

We scratch her name deep in the night's skin,
prick up our ears at each faint mew of the wind.

Sue Wootton

At Night

At night I look up at the sky,
I see the moon and stars sweep by.
I take the universe to bed,
and keep it safe inside my head.

Bill Nagelkerke

Bottled Stars

I shook my
bottle of stars,
and the Milky Way
fizzed over the edge.

Bill Nagelkerke

Whisper to Me

Whisper to me while the spider spins,
sing me a song of seagulls' wings,
tell me the story of sky and hill,
put me to sleep in a paua shell.

Kōhimuhimu mai he rangirangi pūngāwerewere,
waiatatia he oriori parirau karoro,
kōrerotia mai he pūrākau a Rangi, a Nuku,
kia pai ai taku moe i rō anga pāua.

Patricia Grace

The Moon

When everything goes silent,
when the sky dims a darker, deeper shade of blue,
that is when I appear.
I make the sky brighter at night,
I am like a light bulb stuck inside a lampshade.
Although the sun is brighter than me,
I am a smoother,
more gentle light.
For the sun is a furious, flaming ball of fire.
I am calming.
Wolves howl at me when I am full,
they wish they were me,
but I wish I was them.
They have families
that love them.
I am lonely,
but at least I know who I am . . .
I'm the moon.

Becky Reid, aged 12

Night Countdown

There are millions of stars
in the sky tonight
and thousands of lights
on the hill.
There are hundreds of moths
round the thousands of lights
while the air is shining and still.
There are scores of noises
that music the night
and dozens of waves on the sea,
there's a chorus of barking,
a handful of squawks
but
only one moon
and one me.

Peggy Dunstan

From the Hill

At night the town below disappears and in its place
there is a valley of stars gleaming silver and bright.

A valley of silver stars in a circle of hills
— as though a galaxy has fallen out of the skies of night.

Pauline Cartwright

If Stars Were Stitches

If stars were stitches
And the sky a quilt
I'd sew you a patch
On, big and round.

A fat old moon patch
To snuggle you down
And soft light your night
To sleep you sound.

If stars were bright eyes
All winking at us
I'd ask for a smile
Curvy and wide.

A crescent moon boat
To float in the sky
And carry your dreams
On night's high tide.

If stars were diamonds
And the moon a pearl
I'd string them for you
To hang above.

A sparkling necklace
On velvety dark
To wrap around us
My own sweet love.

Melanie Drewery

The Tūī

The tūī is a chortle bird
a chatter bird, a chitter bird, a chuttle bird.

She wears her feather bow
her snowy bow, her foamy bow, her white bow,

on her shining black
her sheeny black, her coal black, her blue black,

in the skinny tree
the spindly tree, the spandly tree, the cabbage tree,

with her gargle song
her giggle song, her glaggle song, her tūī song.

Paula Green

The Fantail Requests

'How can I catch,'
says the wig-wag
zig-zag fantail,
'juicy fat gnats
when your great
head's in the way?
Remember I share,'
chirps the flip-flop
zip-zap fantail,
'with you this air.
So please be fair,'
pipes the flit-flot,
rill-roll fantail,
'and leave me a little
bit of space.'

Bernard Gadd

Threnody

In Plimmerton, in Plimmerton,
The little penguins play,
And one dead albatross was found
At Karehana Bay.

In Plimmerton, in Plimmerton,
The seabirds haunt the cave,
And often in the summertime
The penguins ride the wave.

In Plimmerton, in Plimmerton,
The penguins live, they say,
But one dead albatross they found
In Karehana Bay.

Denis Glover

Where's the Winter Wren

dropping these notes
through the leaves?
one thing I know
she's up there singing
I'm down here saying
where have you gone I wish
you were here there's
so much to tell you so much
we could share so much
these notes have to do

Michele Leggott

The Wind Is Tired of Being Blamed for Everything

The wind wants to be a lizard.
It wants to lie down on a warm rock
with a tiny rustle,
a puff of dust,
and a little flick of the tongue.

The wind wants to be a dog.
It wants to stop when people say so,
it wants to be loved,
it wants to be allowed inside
in bad weather.

Adrienne Jansen

Children's Tale

The taniwha breathes fire
and hot stones.
The taniwha snorts hot dust
and steam.
Golden snot trickles from
his nostrils.

Deep inside the Earth
the taniwha takes deep-breathing
exercises to keep in good shape
for when it has to remind us all
that we are not as powerful as he.

His name is: *RU-AU-MOKO*.
He is the boss of all the taniwhas.

He doesn't give a fart for anyone
or anything. But when he does —
WATCH OUT!

The Earth won't be able to contain
itself.
Earth-mother will split her sides
with laughing.

Hone Tuwhare

The Reluctant Hero, or Barefoot in the Snow

When he put on his socks in the morning
He found they were much too tight.
His feet, without any warning,
Had lengthened over night.
He didn't have any others,
He couldn't pick or choose.
He borrowed a pair of his mother's
And went to put on his shoes.

When he put on his shoes in the morning
He found they were much too tight.
His feet, without any warning,
Had lengthened over night.
His toes and heels were skinned — oh,
His feet had grown like roots.
His shoes went out of the window
And he went to put on his boots.

When he put on his boots in the morning
He found they were much too tight.
His feet, without any warning,
Had lengthened over night.
His little toe was just in,
He had to squash and squeeze.
He threw them into the dust bin
And he went to put on his skis.

When he put on his skis in the morning
He found they were much too tight.
His feet, without any warning,
Had lengthened over night.
He had no footware which in
His feet could feel at ease.
The skis went into the kitchen
And his toes were left to freeze.

And so he went out barefoot,
No socks or shoes he wore.
He trod in places where foot
Had never trod before.
And everywhere his feet sent
A message to the sky.
His footprints down the street meant
A hero's passing by.

Margaret Mahy

Out in the Garden

Out in the garden,
Out in the windy, swinging dark,
Under the trees and over the flower-beds,
Over the grass and under the hedge border,
Someone is sweeping, sweeping,
Some old gardener.
Out in the windy, swinging dark,
Someone is secretly putting in order,
Someone is creeping, creeping.

Katherine Mansfield, written when she was young

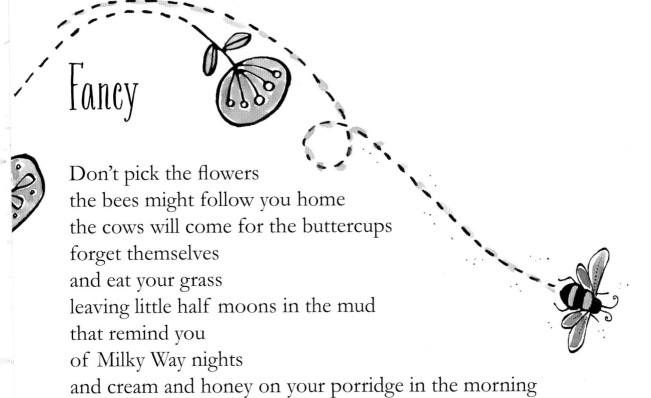

Fancy

Don't pick the flowers
the bees might follow you home
the cows will come for the buttercups
forget themselves
and eat your grass
leaving little half moons in the mud
that remind you
of Milky Way nights
and cream and honey on your porridge in the morning

Melinda Szymanik

Haiku 1

Stop
your snivelling
creek-bed:

come rain hail
and flood-water

laugh again

Hone Tuwhare

Bits and Pieces

Gloves are made with fingers in
to keep out winter weather.
But socks are straight
so all the tocs
are jumbled up together.
I don't know which are better off;
now which would you suppose?
It's warmer for your fingers
but much friendlier
             for toes.

Peggy Dunstan

My Kind of Day

I like a day with a windy whistle
that rips your words away
a blustery gust of a day
that buffets and shoves and shouts in your face

One with an icy blast
to whip and sting your cheeks
that tackles and trips and cheats
pushing you back like a rugby scrum

Then screams you on from behind
roaring a gale
calling your name
as you run, run, run
with a dive for the line

Elena de Roo

Haiku 1

Stop
your snivelling
creek-bed:

come rain hail
and flood-water

laugh again

Hone Tuwhare

The Ferocious Giant

I look out the window
There are trees swaying side to side
Leaves flying towards the sky
Clouds pushing and shoving
Suddenly red eyes pop out, and sharp black
teeth from inside a mouth.
It opens and gets deadlier
There's a bright blur behind the ferocious
giant
It gets smaller and smaller
Whoosh!
Rain drops like a busted water balloon!

Luke Walker, aged 10

Spiders

I'm not scared of spiders.
Spiders are scared of me.
I run away
so they won't have to
run away from me.

Feana Tu'akoi

Haiku

Listlessly on a bare bough
a cicada scrapes
with his bow a few dry notes.

Alistair Te Ariki Campbell

Who Am I?

green leaf
on a tree

flutter, fly
up high

spy make-up
eye wake-up

quick flick
clever trick

circus clown
upside down

twig-clinging
squeaky-singing

often heard
tiny bird

oh my
silver-eye

Claire Gummer

And What Are These?

by your feet
special treats

bright red balls
in a sprawl

hang-dangling
stems tangling

what the heck
take a peck

sticky beak
rosy cheeks

eat 'em raw
back for more

winter loot
ripening fruit

shadow-dappled
crab-apples

Claire Gummer

A Fly

If I could
See this fly
With unprejudiced eye,
I should see his body
Was metallic blue — no,
Peacock blue.
His wings are a frosty puff;
His legs fine wire.
He even has a face,
I notice.
And he breathes, as I do.

Ruth Dallas

The Second-hand Tent

Dad brings it home
in a bright orange sack.

We flip it open —
it starts to chat:

*Sunscreen pipispit
baitstink sandygrit*

*crabscuttle kelp-pop
togs on a guy rope*

*bumblebee lupinsnap
grasswhisper waveslap*

*firecrackle smokesmell
saltbreeze pauashell.*

We sit and listen
with smiles on our faces.

This tent of ours
has places to take us.

Sue Wootton

Red Horse

The red crayon makes us
happiest, selected out with care
and making the outline of a horse
when once it's there complete
a rare delightful business;
then colouring the horse in
red as well, occasionally
going over the edge
but mostly filling up the space
without dismay or panic
and reaching in the box
eyes closed for something more or less
surprising for the sky and finding
deepest blue by accident.

Bill Manhire

Reflections

The lake paints a picture
of the mountains
taking its reflection
and sucking it out
onto the calm morning water.
It's like a photograph,
an exact replica.
The ducks perch
on the water.
It looks like they are
sitting on the very top of
the mountain.

Becky Reid, aged 12

Orowaiti Road

The refuse tip in Westport is a treasure trove
for local school children to explore and forage.

Boys throw flax fronds as light as balsa wood
airplanes fly over the estuary mud flats.

Blue heron stilt walkers tiptoe over the marsh
thousands of Swiss cheese holes bubble and froth.

Pied oystercatchers gossip with gannets
like a knitting circle of old grandmas.

Sunken tyre treads in the stormwater drain
are the fossilised bones of a brontosaurus.

The green glass shards of a broken beer bottle
are polished pounamu in a taniwha's horde.

Girls blow dandelion fairies in the wind
like birthday candles and make a secret wish.

Doc Drumheller

Pukeko

After the rain,
Come the roadside strutters.
Blue shirts and black tails,
Bobbing heads with beady, button eyes.
Foraging for food,
Dancing on spindly, red legs
To an audience of cars.

Madeleine Williams, aged 10

The Veranda View

The grass is waving like a
playground swing

The hills are waves on a stormy sea

The wind is knitting a large green
mat out of the bush

The foam is making a never ending
sheet of rough paper on the surface
of the sea

Henry Eglinton, aged 10

Tuatara

In a country with ridges
up and down its back

lives the tuatara
wearing mountains like the land

moving so slowly
it hardly seems to move at all.

The sun goes whirling
round the world

and winds blow west
and winds blow north

and grasses grow
and trees grow higher

and people come
and they admire

the tuatara sitting still.
It hardly seems to move at all.

Anna Jackson

The Sapling Tree

I
am the sapling
tree.

I
fight my way
upwards.

I
thicken
with my story.

I
house birds
itch cows.

I
am nibbled
& gnawed.

I
am knifed
with names.

I
will outgrow
them.

I
lay down
my winter leaves.

I
leaf again
in sun.

I
am the mighty
sapling tree.

Richard Langston

Skipping Rhyme

Mane, Mane, one, two, three,
Turei, Turei, skip with me.
Wenerei, Wenerei, turn around,
Taite, Taite, touch the ground.
Paraire, Paraire, touch the sky,
Ra Horoi, rope swings high.
Ra Tapu, you're too slow —
End of the week so out you go! (Pepper)

Gwenyth Jones

Ups a Daisy

Ups a daisy Maisie
on the trampoline.
Ups a daisy, ups a daisy,
like a jumping bean.

Bouncing on her bottom,
flipping to her feet.
Rising like a rocket
in the noonday heat.

Still she keeps on bouncing
all the afternoon.
High above the tree tops,
tries to touch the moon.

Ups a daisy, ups a daisy,
bounces up too far.
Ups a daisy Maisie
is now a shooting star.

Gwenyth Jones

Dragons

Dragons are playful, dragons eat sushi
Dragons are evil, they are as red as lava
Dragons are destructive, they can do anything
Dragons can destroy buildings, skyscrapers and the Great
Wall of China

Charlie Aubrey, aged 7

Dragons

Dragons are big
Dashing around in the sky
Swooping down
To the mountains
Breathing fire everywhere
Then landing in their lairs
On huge piles of gold
With a big thump!

Nathan Hodge, aged 9

The Vagabond Tomato

I'm a juicy red tomato
and I've tumbled off the shelf
and I'm rolling out the co-op door
to the street, all by myself.

I've left the other fruit behind
but I feel no remorse.
There's more to life than waiting
to be blended into sauce
or chopped up for a pizza
or sliced to serve with ham
or just sitting, going mouldy,
fifty cents a kilogram.

No, no! Heigh ho for the open road
and the footpath, wild and free!
Where feet pass by
'neath an open sky
and there are no other veggies but me!

You won't catch me in your casserole
or your pyrex baking dish.
I'm the vagabond tomato and I'm . . .

gurgle gurgle squish

Fiona Farrell

Fake Blood

Like a cookbook
recipe, they mix
maple syrup and red
food colouring.
Stir well.
Shake before use.

But this is no
sauce — this is the source
of blood to be burst
from its bag on cue.

When the 'bullet' fires,
they pull the wires.
Bang! Snap! Splatter!
Bang! Snap! Splatter!

Wearing the safety harness
you'll never see,
the villain, covered
in fake blood,
falls from the edge
of a high building ledge . . .

Jenny Powell

Scaly Tail the Rat

I'm Scaly Tail the Rat I am
As quick as any cat I am
A most malignant rat I am
Beware my pitter pat
In tunnels dark and dungeons cold
In cells and sewers thick with mould
You'll hear my footsteps fleet and bold
It's Scaly Tail the Rat

I'm Scaly Tail the plump I am
A sight to make you jump I am
And dirty as a dump I am
While silent as a bat
A wicked eye amid the dark
A shadow scurries swift and stark
The tooth and claw to leave the mark
Of Scaly Tail the Rat

I'm Scaly Tail the beast I am
Unwanted at your feast I am
Though Prince of rats at least I am
And confident in stating
When final conflict strips your states
When decency disintegrates
Thy kingdom comes for one who waits
It's Scaly Tail — I'm waiting.

Jon Gadsby

119

Mr Nelligan's Nightshirt

Old Mr Nelligan's nightshirt
Has tigers all over the place.
In jungle of green they are crouching,
All growly and scowling of face.
They seem to be watching and waiting
For someone to walk the dark track
That makes its way right down the middle
Of old Mr Nelligan's back.
He doesn't know as he potters
At making his toast and his tea,
Those tigers that crouch on his nightshirt
Are hungrily staring at me!

Shirley Gawith

What My Dragon Likes

What my dragon likes for breakfast,
The minute that it wakes,
Is a bowl of battery acid,
And a stack of T-bone steaks.

What my dragon likes for supper,
The final thing at night,
Is a drum of oil, a sack of coal,
And a stick of dynamite.

Greg O'Connell

Monsters

Monsters with horns
monsters with thorns
monsters all prickly and
stickly and scaly and
green gristly taily.

Don't turn your back,
don't close your eyes;
monsters can hide
in a box or a crack.

Monsters all purply
monsters all slurply
monsters all spotty and
frothy and growly and
claw-footed prowly.

Don't turn your back,
don't close your eyes;
monsters can hide
in a box or a crack.

Make the monsters
at home with a bed,
TV and shower
and keep them well fed;
and perhaps they'll grow friendly

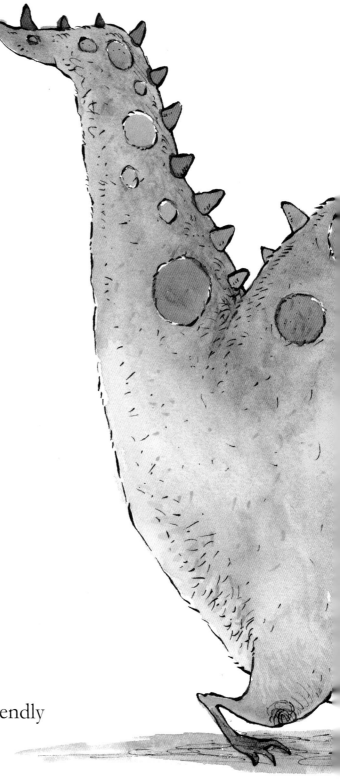

and less frightening horrendly
and two little boys
can play safely instead.

Helen Jacobs

Raisin' Chickens

When,
my granny lived out west,
she wished on a chicken bone.
She closed her eyes and prayed,
her chickens would come home.

You see,
they'd been away all night,
painting the town bright red.
'Twas time they all came home,
and got themselves to bed.

Heavens,
they had to get up early.
There were lots of eggs to lay,
had to tidy up their nests,
there was no time to play.

They had to,
lay eggs for Granny's breakfast,
lay eggs for Granny's lunch,
lay eggs to sell at market
to give the cakes some punch.

But,
as soon as the sun went down,
those chooks got gussied up,
and took themselves to town
to drink, to dance, and sup.

And,
they danced the hoochie koochie,
threw their legs into the air,
gave no thought to tomorrow
and the eggs they'd have to bear.

Yes,
they shimmied through the night
till dawn came through the door.
Then they gathered up their skirts —
it was time to hit the straw.

Then,
all day those chookies slumbered,
not one egg did they lay.
Their nests, unmade and messy —
unruly heaps of hay.

There were,
no eggs for Granny's breakfast,
no eggs for Granny's lunch,
no eggs to sell at market
to give the cakes some punch.

Then,
as soon as the sun went down,
those chooks got gussied up.
They were aimin' to go to town
to drink, to dance, and sup.

But,
my sly old Gran was ready,
she stood out by the gate,
clutchin' her old leaf blower —
her hurr'cane-force playmate.

And,
she blew those chookies sideways,
she blew them off their feet,
fancy frocks were blown off,
and tossed about the street.

Yes,
Gran blew the hens into the coop
and snibbed the door real tight.
'Old hens dressed up as chickens
are not a pretty sight.'

Inside,
she went up to her bedroom
and opened the wardrobe door.
There hung a dazzling, feathered dress,
with sparkles to the floor.

Quickly,
she slipped into the garment
and pushed her hair up high,
painted her lips bright carmine
to catch a varmint's eye.

And,
her high heels made a clatter
as she hurried down the steps.
Across the yard she swaggered,
swinging her glittery hips.

She called,
'Nighty night you suckers,
I'm off to the honky-tonk.
It's my turn now to party,
to dance and drink some plonk.'

Next morning,
there were eggs for Granny's breakfast,
there were eggs for Granny's lunch,
there were eggs to sell at market
to give the cakes some punch.

But,
no one came to collect them.
They lay without a peep,
just like granny in her bed,
all tuckered out, asleep.

Yes, when,
my granny lived out west,
she did two things very well —
raisin' chickens, she did best,
but she was better — raisin' hell.

Gavin Bishop

Rhymes

Let's start with jelly.
It's a wobbly word
that rhymes with belly
and smelly of course
and my old Aunt Nelly
who's also wobbly
and works in a deli
when she's not at home
in front of the telly
being wobbly and eating jelly
and thinking of her brother Kelly
who ran away with a girl called Shelly
who worked — small world —
in the very same deli
as wobbly telly-loving
old Aunt Nelly.
Rhymes run around
as light as a feather.
Think of a few
and put them together!

Peter Bland

The Dictionary Bird

Through my house in sunny weather
Flies the Dictionary Bird
Clear to see on every feather
Is some outlandish word.

'Hugger Mugger' 'gimcrack' 'guava'
'Waggish' 'mizzle' 'swashing rain'
Bird — fly back into my kitchen,
Let me read those words again.

Margaret Mahy

Mr Swash

He swallows the shirts, he swallows the socks,
He swallows the hankies, the pants, and the frocks.

The soap goes splish! the water goes splosh!
And they all hold hands in a splish-splosh wash.

He glugs and he gurgles, he rinses and swirls,
Then faster and faster he spins and he twirls.

Then Mr Swash beeps, to say, 'All done!
Please take them out to dance in the sun!'

John Parker

Elephap Rap

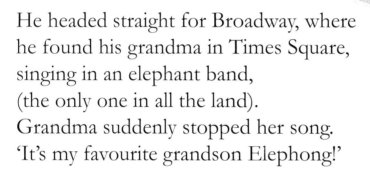

Now everybody knows you can't
find words to rhyme with elephant,
so here's a different kind of rhyme
about a brave young elephyme
who set out on a long, long walk
to see his grandma in New York.

He headed straight for Broadway, where
he found his grandma in Times Square,
singing in an elephant band,
(the only one in all the land).
Grandma suddenly stopped her song.
'It's my favourite grandson Elephong!'

What a warm welcome the youngster got
from this cheerful band of elephot.
'Come and join our show!' they cried.
'Are you a musical elephied?
Can you warble? Can you hum?
Can you play the guitar or drum?'

So the grandson joined the elephant band
and became a musical elephand.
Now animals travel from near and far
to hear this new young elephant star,
and everyone stands to cheer and clap
when he trumpets that Broadway Elephap Rap.

Joy Cowley

Wet Spell

Hurricane eye and peal of thunder,
drizzle of the spit of a dew-damp spider,
end of a rainbow swizzled in the sea,
red cloud squeezed through a dark blue breeze.

Dragon tear — saltless; clown tear — pink.
Blend in a tablespoon of cuttlefish ink.
Storm in a tea cup, stir in the steam,
add seven bubbles from a bush-fringed stream.

Wet spell, strong spell. Too strong! Long spell.
Three days rain fell. Wet sock pong smell.
Stuck in the classroom, can't run about,
brawling and bawling makes the teacher shout.

Scrawl on the window and peer through the glass.
Plink. Plonk. Plink. Puddles on the grass.
Tick. Tock. Tick. Time crawls, time stalls . . .

                              walls
                         the
                    climbing
              are
         snails
      the
Even

Sue Wootton

The Gentle Rain

The rain the rain the gentle rain
Falls upon the streets again
And falls upon the country where
Top-dressing dust still haunts the air.

The rain is soft the rain is gentle
It loves the umbrella and the mantle
And when it falls it brings delight
To flowers and weeds and streets alike.

It gives our raincoat jobs to do
And tests anew the well-soled shoe.
It falls on car on bus on train
I know I like the gentle rain

When I am well wrapped-up. Don't you?

Denis Glover

Windscreen Wiper

Flicker flicker flack!
Flicker flicker flack!
The wiper on the car goes
Flicker flicker flack.
The rain falls flick!
And the rain falls flack!
And the wiper on the car goes
Flicker flicker flack!
Flick!
Flack!

S K Vickery

Leap Frog

This pond
like
a mirror
reflects
the sky.

A frog breaks the surface
leaps high
above the sun
and falls
back into
a sea of clouds.

Apirana Taylor

The Braid of Rivers

I wear a braid of rivers.
It has carved a riverbed
in my spine, and as I walk

the braid of rivers thumps my back.
By day I wear a voluminous hat
to keep it tucked away. At nights

I let it loose, the braid of rivers, and it pours
down the pebbles of my vertebrae
reciting the names of its plaits.

Whanganui, Rangitikei, Tongariro.
Waitaki, Taieri, Waikouaiti.
Clutha, Kawarau, Manuherikia.

Sue Wootton

Rain

I can hear you
making small holes
in the silence
rain

If I were deaf
the pores of my skin
would open to you
and shut

And I
should know you
by the lick of you
if I were blind

the something
special smell of you
when the sun cakes
the ground

the steady
drum-roll sound
you make
when the wind drops

But if I
should not hear
smell or feel or see
you

you would still
define me
disperse me
wash over me
rain

Hone Tuwhare

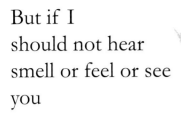

Autumn

Leaves flutter to the ground
Trees stripped of their coverings
They lie like a fiery blanket on the ground
Crunched to crumbs by my feet

Amanda MacDonald-Keepa, aged 10

Huri Huri

huri huri turn turn
turn turn wiri wiri
huri huri huri huri
wiri wiri turn turn
the wind blows
wiri wiri blows
the wind huri
huri wiri wiri turn
turn the leaves
fall turn turn
huri huri wiri wiri

Apirana Taylor

Dogwobble

doga   doga

wobble bark wobble bark
wobble wobble bark wag wobble wobble
wag wag wobble bark wag
wobble wag wag wobble wobble
bark bark wobble wag
one two three a
doga doga doga doga doga doga doga doga
wag dog wobble wobble
one two three a
jellyfish dog in a toothbrush tree.

Cilla McQueen

wobble

wobble

wobble

bark

bark

W o o f

w o o f

w o b b l e

w o b b l e

b a r k

The Bonnet Macaque: An Omnivore

What does the bonnet macaque
keep in her cheek pocket?
Does she store the rocky shore
a dining-room table and the horse's stable
comic books and clucking chooks
basketballs and outlandish fools
DVDs and TVs
snowboards and Aunt Maude
lollipops and circus flops
snorkelling gear and a grizzly bear
sharp scooters and football hooters?

There's no couch in her cheek pouch
for in her larder for a starter
she hoards a one-stop shop,
luscious food for every mood.

Paula Green

Jellyfish

I am a blubber jellyfish
A bendy rubber belly fish.
I swim upon the ocean tides
You can see through my insides.
I have a shrink wrap sort of skin
A bag to keep my body in.
Umbrella-like I move about
Suck in water, let it out.
I wear a skirt edged with lace
I curtsy, dip and move with grace —
When my kinfolk cluster near
We sparkle like a chandelier.
I drift about the frothy sea
A glassy disc floating free.
When you see me on the shore
Leave me for the ocean's roar.
I think you'll find that if you do
I'll opal into ocean blue.

Stephanie Mayne

Snorkelling

I'm travelling with turtles
down deep in the sea
down where it's silent
nothing but me

only the green
of the sun shafted sea
and the touch of a turtle shell
brushing by me

Elena de Roo

Skin-diving

I slink below
this shiny blue skin
and I see the water
winking.

Help!
Kelp!
Straps
of vegetable leather
slap and shove
and hassle
the rocks and me —
I'm in a submarine
car-wash.

Rachel McAlpine

Sea Creatures

The flounder
flounders,
eels
feel;
sharks
can bark
and goatfish
kneel.

Some people
watch
as perch
search,
snapper
flatter
and batfish
bounce;

but out on the coral
deep in the night
nobody sees
the moonfish's light,
nobody knows
the secret glitter
that turns to silver
the darkened water.

Lauris Edmond

Further Adventures of Humpty Dumpty

Humpty Dumpty, King of the Eggs,
Ran down the road on his little short legs.
After him, quickly, came forty-two cooks
Who lived in a castle of cookery books,
Charging and barging the length of the street,
Holding their egg beaters ready to beat,
Shouting out 'Omelettes!' and 'Scrambled!' as well.
What a terrible shock for a king in a shell!

Margaret Mahy

Joshua Jones

Joshua Jones was a spinning boy.
He whirled and twirled like a frenzied toy.
'Joshua,' his mother would sadly say,
'You'll spin off the edge of the world one day.'
And one day, suddenly
      off he went
with his arms stretched out and his head all bent.
Circling the city he spun away
right over the hills
at the end of the day,
humming a tune for the world to hear,
the moon at his elbow
the pale stars near . . .

Peggy Dunstan

The Alien

The spiky cabbage tree
looks like an alien from Mars
standing alone in a field
not knowing what to do
or how to speak the language.
The cows are just mooching
around in the paddock
eating grass.

Laura Ranger, written when she was 8

A Witch in the Sky

There's a witch in the sky she's whirling
& twirling like a lonely cylinder in the sky
She's twittering & talking

She's flying she's scheming she's out & about
Again!

She's swooping, she's looping
She's all about, she's everywhere!

She's swooshing like a cheetah in the air!
Oh no, here she comes to capture me!

Sofia Pawley, aged 8

Jet-whales

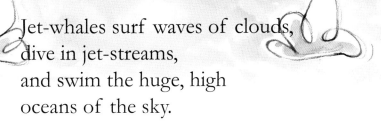

I think that jet-planes
have tails
like whales.

Jet-whales surf waves of clouds,
dive in jet-streams,
and swim the huge, high
oceans of the sky.

Sometimes they trail a white wake
as they make
their piercing jet-whale song.

Even when they've gone
I hear them singing,
singing strong and long,
strong and long.

John Parker

Wild Ideas

They're wild, my ideas.
You can watch them run, but there's no way
you could ride them. I sit on the fence
in my head. I don't dare go near them.
I've tried taking them
by surprise — creeping up, hardly breathing,
till I'm certain
they're not looking. 'Is this another
of your wild ideas?' my dad groans, and I know
what he's thinking: wild ideas
won't get you anywhere.
But I'd love to leap
on the back of the wildest one,
squeeze my eyes shut,
and gallop into the unknown.
Where do wild ideas go
when they're galloping home?

Ashleigh Young

The Night Kite

I flew our house
The other night.
It makes a lovely
Bright box-kite.

Like a big square moon
It slowly rose
Tied to a reel
Of garden hose.

As for the tail . . .
I'd had the sense
To borrow a length
Of our front fence.

It floated all night
Above our back lawn
While my sister sneezed
And my brother snored.

What shall I tell them
When they awake
About hoses that float
And houses in space?

I'll tell them nothing.
It wouldn't make sense.
I'll just reel in that hose
And sit on the fence.

Peter Bland

Sparkle

The sun leaves only a golden sigh
in the drowning blue of the bottomless sky.
Bicycles spin, moths take flight,
cicadas kiss in the sunken light.
Runaway feet spill down the street —
and into the unknown night.

Out after bedtime, out after dark,
mad as mosquitoes they race to the park.
Snippets of song skate on the breeze,
tangling in lanterns, hanging from trees.
Children are humming, jittering, thrumming —
as onto the stage they squeeze.

An audience gathers on makeshift seats.
Quickening bones, a bass drum beats.
A violin moans, a flute takes wing,
the choir shifts like an alien thing.
Hot shiny faces seeking out places —
tilting up skyward to sing.

Eyes on the teacher, ears hear the note,
feet start to stamp, sounds start to float.
Snapping out fast bits, shuffling through slow,
stretching for high bits, looping for low.
Voices entwine, swagger and shine —
as higher and louder they go.

They conjure a trick with the sounds they share —
a palace of notes in the cool night air!
See how it gleams! See-through and bright,
see there a window, a stairway, a light.
Gone are the scars of these raggedy stars
aglow in the indigo night.

And then there is silence.
An echo abrupt . . .
till stamping and shouting and clapping erupt!
A hug, a handshake, kindnesses said.
The concert is done, a long walk ahead.
Humming new tunes
in the light of the moon,
they carry their smiles
to bed.

Ruth Paul

Mary, Mary

Mary, Mary, from Jackson's dairy,
how does your garden grow?
With kowhai bells and paua shells,
and painted white tyres in a row.

Peter Millett

Goldfish

What's it like to have a goldfish
Not a flounder or a sole fish
But a swimming-round-a-bowl fish
For a friend and for a pet?
Because it's different from a flatfish
Or a thin fish, or a fat fish
And I wouldn't want a catfish
'Cause they don't like getting wet

Yes I'd rather have a goldfish
I don't care if it's an old fish
But it shouldn't be a cold fish
Should be warm and bright and gold
Not a catch-it-in-a-net fish
But a cuddly little wet fish
Though it's sort of hard to pet fish
'Cause they're difficult to hold

When you watch a kitten clawing
Or a puppy always gnawing
You might think a goldfish boring
But it's not like that at all
Though a goldfish doesn't do much
Doesn't bite and scratch and chew much
Well, you don't expect it to much —
It's a goldfish, after all.

Jon Gadsby

Outstanding Outside

What I like about the outside are the birds chirping in harmony
What I hate about the outside is when I fall on my knee

What I love about the outside is the whisper of leaves
What I hate about the outside is the CRASH of falling trees

What I like about the outside is the shine of the summer sun
What I hate about the outside is when there is no more fun

What I love about the outside is the crash of the waves
What I hate about the outside are the big concrete paves

Skye Atkins, aged 8

First You Get the Knives and Forks

I love it
when my Aunty Mabel
asks me to help her
set the table.

'First let's find
the knives and forks,'
but I *thought* she said
the knives and *storks*!

I searched the kitchen
upside down
but there were NO storks
to be found!

'Next put out
the tomato sauce,'
but I *thought* she said
tomato *horse*!

Perhaps my silly
Aunty Mabel
thought her kitchen
was a stable!

I searched here
and I searched there
but there was no horse
anywhere!

'Now let's put out
the cups and saucers,'
but I *thought* she said
the *topsy tortoise*!

I ran about
in a hopeless circle
there wasn't even
a topsy *turtle*!

'Now can you find
the salt and pepper?'
But I *thought* she said
the *spotted leopard*!

A spotted leopard?
Fancy that!
All I could find
was a stripy cat.

'I think we need
some paper towels.'
But I *thought* she said
some *guinea fowls*!

I opened cupboards
I pulled out drawers,
flung open windows
threw open doors!

I saw Aunty Mabel
in her pinny
but not a single fowl
from Guinea!

'Perhaps we'll need
some apple juice,'
but I *thought* she said
a *dappled moose*!

Of course I couldn't
find a moose
in a box
or on the loose,

I said 'Dear Aunty
wouldn't you
rather have
a kangaroo?'

She looked at me
with great surprise
took off her glasses
rubbed her eyes.

'Why would I want
a kangaroo?
We're making tea dear
not a zoo!'

James Norcliffe

Spring-heeled Jack

Spring-heeled Jack
Jumped up and down
Higher than anyone
Else in the town.

The heels of his boots
Were fitted with springs;
He could fly
Like a bird with wings.

The first time up
He jumped so high
He made thunder
In the sky.

The second time up
He jumped far higher —
The North Wind set
His coat on fire.

The third time up
He jumped with zest —
The eagles plucked
His hair for a nest.

But the very last time
Spring-heeled Jack
Jumped to the moon
And never came back.

James K Baxter

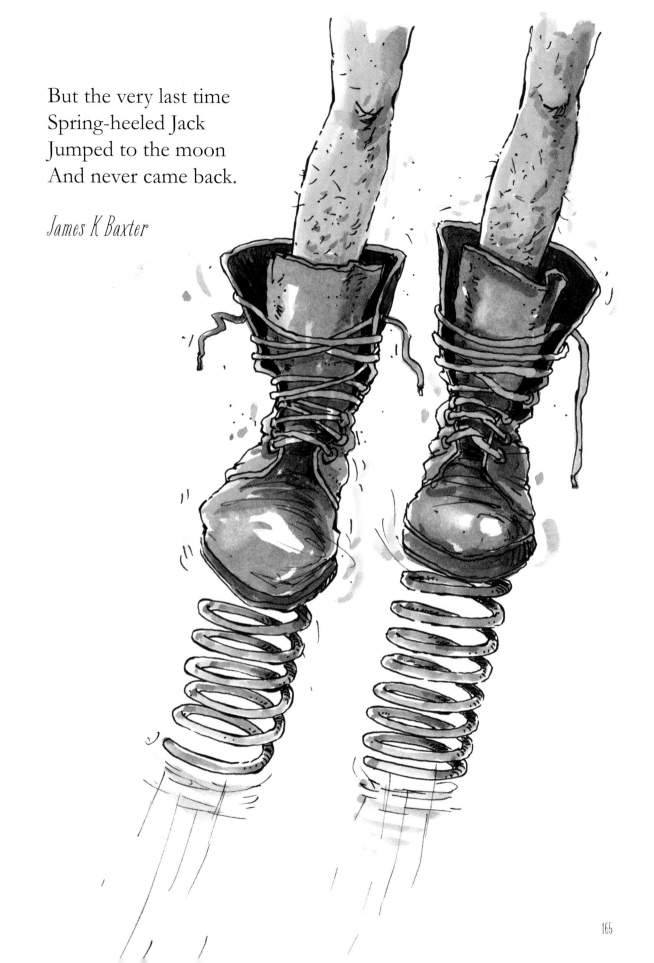

If You Feel Blue, Get on Your Ski-doo

If you feel blue, get on your ski-doo
And swiffle your way through the snow.
Ski-dare to be bold, even though it is cold!
Ski-don't let it lay you low!

Ski-daddle along, singing a song,
Ski-do what has got to be done!
Your heart will ski-dance at each fabulous chance,
And ski-dart with delight at the fun.

Margaret Mahy

Fried, Please

Sometimes in winter, from the top of my cliff,
When the day is still and clear,
I think the sea is the world's biggest frying-pan,
With the world's biggest handle sticking out
Somewhere in space.

And all day the frying-pan rocks and sways,
This way and that,
Trying to catch the world's biggest egg.
Lower and lower slides the egg,
Lower and
Lower.
Then it drops into the frying-pan.
The egg bubbles red.

Time for tea.

John Parker

A Chinese Song

Our mother sings
a Chinese song
as she works in the kitchen
all day long.

She rises early
to make our breakfast
rice porridge pickles boiled eggs
milk and slices of fresh bread.

For lunch she cooks ribbon noodles
in a hot broth with Chinese greens
picked from the garden
and rinsed through a sieve.
She adds thin slices of barbecue pork
spring onions and bean sprouts on top.

In the afternoon a yeasty aroma fills the air.
Our mother makes Chinese buns
kneading the dough
counting the pieces like little children.
She rolls them pats them
shapes and stuffs them
with sweet and savoury fillings.
She makes dumplings
her nimble fingers neatly
pleating tiny purses.

She puts them into a large pot
steams the dumplings till they're piping hot
then serves them with fragrant tea
in white china cups.

In the evening our mother washes rice
rubbing the grains through her fingers
in a rhythmic circular motion.
She stir fries vegetables
carrots broccoli celery
sweet red and yellow peppers.
She marinates sliced meat
in garlic ginger and spicy sauce
then cooks it over a fiery heat.
The wok sizzles and sighs
as she tosses and turns the ingredients.
We smell the food we love to eat.

Our mother sings
a Chinese song
as she works in the kitchen
all day long.

Belinda Wong

Kai 'Umu

Food
buried
way down deep
on stones warmed by
slow-burning embers,
cooked slowly for
maximum
flavour.
YUM!

Feana Tu'akoi

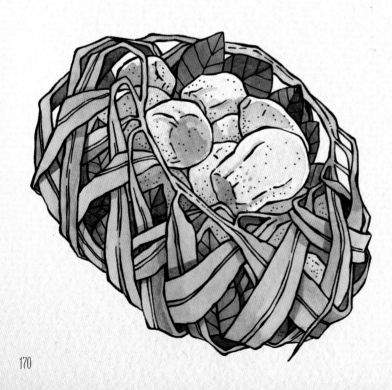

Did You Ever?

Did you ever
watch the fireworks in
your backyard
sizzling crackling booming bright
exploding into a million specks
flying through the air
like a meteorite
as bright as the sun?
It's tremendous!

Mac van den Heuvel, aged 9

# Christmas 1953

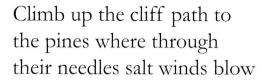

Climb up the cliff path to
the pines where through
their needles salt winds blow

and far below
the fish and ocean go

and down the cliff path home
bring a lone
Christmas tree

and by the beach
let it in warm winds grow.

Sam Hunt, written when he was 7

Christmas Festival

We went for a long holiday this Christmas.
While we were away, thousands of colourful flowers
sprouted, covering our lawn like festive decorations —
rustling grass streamers, clover balls, and daisy stars.
Ours was the most interesting lawn in the neighbourhood.
I thought it beautiful, but Dad was aghast!
Before even a day had passed he'd mown them down
and, like our holiday, their festival did not last.

Anne McDonell

The Cat of Habit

The cat of habit
knows the place by heart
or at least by space, scent, direction, bulk,
by shadow and light
moonlight starlight sunlight
and where to nest in each
with a three-focussed shut eye
on who or what's coming and going
on the earth and in the sky
and distantly, not present, the rays of inkling
shining within the furred skull.

The cat of habit curls her spine
in the most windless the most warm place
shivering a little with, 'It's mine',
an ear-twitch, tail-flip
of permanent ownership.

The cat of habit
has the place marked,
the joint cased.

Feed and sleep and feed
and half-heartedly catch
moths and mice and mostly watch
hourlong for the passing witch
for many, unseen, pass
through the rooms of the house and outside,
under the trees and in the grass.

Janet Frame

Giddy

You say *giddy*
giddy giddy giddy
giddy and very soon
you are and you fall
right down.

Jenny Bornholdt

Garden 5

For Caleb Alualu

Every time Caleb our 8-year-old mokopuna   stays with us
he tries to win Mānoa's affection but she won't have any of it
For the last two days his father has pruned and cut down some of
our overgrown trees while three teenage mokopuna and I piled up
the cut trunks   branches   and foliage into a large maze pungent with
drying timber and leaves   which Mānoa explored   oblivious to
Caleb's desperate attempts to befriend her
My daughter Sina came for morning tea on the lānai: coffee crispies and
fruit mince pies while Caleb tracked the heartless Mānoa through the maze
The sun hid behind a mattress of milk-white cloud that stretched over
the city and up to Waitakere and refused to help Caleb

Reina keeps telling him the next time he comes Mānoa won't spurn
his alofa: cats are cats and you just have to wait for them to trust you
Unlike humans they're very honest about their feelings

Albert Wendt

Just for the Record

When teacher lets the stylus down
And round and round the record goes
Up comes a poet's thinking frown
A poet's choosy nose.

Oh children, do you hear me groan?
Your faces all are shiny new.
Once I was beautiful like you,
Now I'm a voice on the gramophone.

C K Stead

Nana's Painting

I see the dark shapes of the hills
on the horizon,
the man in his kayak,
and the setting sun,
which is reflected in the mirror-like water
as the rest of the sky is.
Orange over blue.
The sun is peering out from behind the hills,
trying to maintain its reflection,
but is being pushed down by the night.

If you look closely you can see her
signature in the bottom right corner.

Anne-Marie Groves, aged 10

Finding a Poem

I feel there's a poem calling me in a stale room.
I can't presume,
but if I could get at it,
give it air,
it might dance like a butterfly,
sing like a forest of bellbirds,
prance like a unicorn,
sting like a bee —

but the front door's locked,
and rattling the knob won't do it for me.

The back door's shut, too.

There's no key under the mat.

As I wonder what to do
I sense a pair of eyes.
I'm being observed by a skinny cat,
sitting on a brown wooden fence.

It watches me try round the house.
Maybe there's an open window?
A gap to squeeze through?
A point of entry?

No.
So I turn to go —
then the cat rubs hard against my leg, purring.
Its green eyes stare at me, unblinking.
Suddenly a stirring —
is this the poem I've been searching for?

John Parker

A Swan Plant in the Kitchen

In the corner of the kitchen
lives our friend Cheese-and-whiskers

on the swan plant where he hatched out
of his egg, a tiny caterpillar.

Cheese-and-whiskers is filling out,
processing leaf into stripes.

He drapes himself over a leaf
like a dress thrown over a chair.

And then another egg hatches
and here is Stripy, clinging on

underneath the same leaf, like
a thread of cotton clinging to a hem.

Now Cheese-and-whiskers is an umbrella handle,
now the spout of a teapot,

while Stripy is grazing her leaf
into lacework — a doily.

Cheese-and-whiskers just hangs around,
till one day we find him turning leaf-green again,

turning into a globe.
Ten days later, he comes out —

wet at first, but stripy again, he flutters
around like a frock on a washing line.

And Stripy has grown matronly.
She folds herself up like a towel.

Soon she'll be smooth and green
as a smooth green soap

before she, too, comes out again
to hang her wings out to dry.

Anna Jackson

The Old Bull

On the edge of town
in a paddock summer brown
the old bull stands alone
watching the cars whiz by
with their coats shining, their horns
honking silly tunes, their eyes intense, glaring,
part of a brightly coloured herd roaming
freely to everywhere and anywhere at faster speed
than ever the old bull had.

The old bull drinks at the rusted watertank.
He blinks his bloodshot eyes.
He swishes his tail at the blowflies.
He grunts, snorts, watches a while
the young herd of bullocks
futureless in the paddocks
on the edge of town
near the brick units and the new Rest Home.

Neither happy nor sad
the old bull just being and standing
like a piece of used furniture
old oak ready to whiten in the sun
old oak, old bull
pride of the farm
of the farmer who grew old
who said, I'll subdivide

the farm on the edge of town
and the old bull and I will stand side by side,
he in his paddock
I in my unit of brick
watching the herd of traffic.

Janet Frame

Rain on the Roof

I love to hear the rain
   When I am snug in bed,
As loud as the roar of a train
   On the roof overhead.
    I love to hear the rain.

I love to hear the wind blowing
   Through tussocks or pines,
Around the corners of houses going,
   Or whistling in telegraph lines.
    I love to hear the wind blowing.

Ruth Dallas

the farm on the edge of town
and the old bull and I will stand side by side,
he in his paddock
I in my unit of brick
watching the herd of traffic.

Janet Frame

In Other Words

A poem is a way
of knowing you are alive

As shocking as a fish
leaping out of deep water

As sharp as light stabbing
through a row of trees

As bold as opening up
your eyes during prayer

As simple as lying awake
in the middle of the night
listening to the sound
of people snoring

Every minute
of every day
of every life

is a full library

Glenn Colquhoun

Seasons

A tree grows by our gate.

In winter
It's a black skeleton.

In spring
It's a white bonfire.

In summer
It's a green galaxy.

In autumn
It's golden rain.

A tree **glows** by our gate.

David Hill

Ice Trolls

In winter there must still be trolls under the ice.
I'll skate the lines
I'd send to them,
not looking out the corner
of my eye while I write
these lines to my trolls in the ice.

In spring there must still be yeti in the snow.
I'll think of them
far out of reach, and know
it's just the blossom from the apple tree
that's tapping on my shoulder
like a code.

In summer I hear mermaids in the sea
sing to me,
their long-limbed daughter,
hearing things I do not know I'm saying
in the swaying
of my hair under the water.

In autumn the dark comes lowering
itself down early, gently.
Sky-soft,
wind-sore,
the year is nearly over.
Only my trolls stay awake, waiting for the ice.

Anna Jackson

Rain on the Roof

I love to hear the rain
  When I am snug in bed,
As loud as the roar of a train
  On the roof overhead.
    I love to hear the rain.

I love to hear the wind blowing
  Through tussocks or pines,
Around the corners of houses going,
  Or whistling in telegraph lines.
    I love to hear the wind blowing.

Ruth Dallas

We Could Just Disappear

We disappear,
ten carriages of us,
a tunnel as long as
tomorrow, next term,
a tunnel as long as next year,
as long as time.

No one knows when
we will come out the other end —
we could go on and on and
on forever and never
come out again.
We could just disappear.

Sam Hunt

Washday for the Clouds

The sky is drying
his shape-changing sheets
on the west wind today.

He rinsed the sheets
last night, and pounded them
on the thunder stones.

Tomorrow, when the sheets have aired,
there will be dragons
and castles in the sky.

Bev Kemp

Soapsuds

When I am in my bath at night
The soapsuds give me much delight;
They float about like bits of lace . . .
I love to put them on my face.
And little boats like ships at sea
Come sailing up the bath to me.
Sometimes they bring the sweetest things —
White feathers from a seagull's wings,
And pretty little silver scales
That might have come from mermaids' tails.

Gloria Rawlinson, written when she was young

Old Man Wind

Old man wind
You've been blowing for a while now
Telling stories of angry pirates
That can't fight your breath

Old man wind
With billowing pants
And hair that moves
North south east and west

Old man wind
With sleepless eyes
And puckered lips

Old man thief
Give me back my hat

Tamsin Flynn

Kick-off

The boot wants to be the flag,
    high on the goalposts,
The flag wants to be the whistle,
    commanding respect,
The whistle wants to be the hand,
    scoring the final try,
The hand wants to be the foot,
    landing the winning conversion,
The foot wants to be the ball,
    the centre of attention,
The ball wants to be the lineout,
    reaching for the sky,
The lineout wants to be the scrum,
    crouching on solid ground,
The scrum wants to be the referee,
    letting the game flow,
The referee wants to be the captain,
    holding up the trophy,
The captain wants to be the team,
    standing united,
The team wants to be the crowd,
    doing the Mexican Wave,
The crowd wants to be the boot,
    kicking things off . . .

Greg O'Connell

Whanganui-a-tara

The dragon dips
  his head
to drink

where taniwha
  once
escaped to sea.

It has scales
  of glass
and steel,

breathes sodium
  in the night,
smokes the water.

Angels shaped from
  halogen
mourn till daybreak,

then flicker heavenward
 drawing their
wings like clouds

around them.

Phil Kawana

Haka

when i hear the haka
i feel it in my bones
and in my wairua
the call of my tipuna
flashes like lightning
up and down my spine
it makes my eyes roll
and my tongue flick
it is the dance
of earth and sky
the rising sun
and the earth shaking
it is the first breath of life
eeeee aaa ha haaa

Apirana Taylor

Cloud

cloud is
a playful thing
conjured up a rabbit
from a hat a doodle
on white paper a bubble
above your head think
a concrete poem an alien
vehicle an eyeball a dance
and sometimes cloud is
a serious thing a hive buzzing
with electricity black ice
surprise climate change signal
a symphony pianissimo see
its movement leaves you spellbound
and sometimes it is just cloud
raining raining raining raining

/   /   /   /   /   /   /
/   /   /   /   /   /   /
/   /   /   /   /   /   /
/   /   /   /   /   /   /

Siobhan Harvey

Storm

A storm is·coming.
The hot wind carries
a whisper of thunder.
The trees are anxious.
They call to one another,
'Wrap up tight!
Hold on to your leaves!'
The wind is changing.
Fat, chilly puffs squeeze
under the door.
'The cold is coming,' they shriek
through the cracks in the floor.
The chimney roars,
'Light the fire! Light the fire!'
Then the sky cracks open.

Terrie Huege de Serville

My Cat

My cat
becomes a tiger.
His eyes are
wide and bright.
He shimmers
in the shadows,
then melts
into the night.

Alan Bagnall

Out in the Night Time

Out in the night time,
In a hole in a tree,
Lived an old mother morepork,
And her little ruru three.

'Morepork,' said the mother,
'Morepork,' said the three,
So they moreporked all night,
In a hole in a tree.

Melanie Drewery

morepork
morepork
morepork
morepork

Nanny

Ae, Nanny. I loved holidays with you . . .

Boiling pots of crayfish with legs
orangely poking under lids,
and steaming bowls of pork bones
slurped in soupy watercress.

Ae, Nanny, and the cockles
spitting sea when they opened on the fire,
and the black-lipped paua
blistering in butter.

You speared the skid of flounder
in pepperings of sand
down at the lagoon,
and I ate them for breakfast,
sizzle singing on my plate.

Louise Tomlinson

Pāua

Swirls of pink
like Nanny's rosy cheeks,
one side as smooth as
the pounamu around my neck,
rough on the other
like Koro's big hands.

The smell of the ocean
takes my mind
back to the East Coast beach
where beauty stands still,
like my precious pāua
perched on the window sill.

Nadia Moon, Whānau-a-Apanui

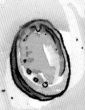

Rain

I like the straight-down,
      Silky rain,
The fat, warm drops
    Of summer rain;
But not the sideways,
      Driving rain,
That stinging, sharp
    Midwinter rain.

Bill Nagelkerke

The Scarf

Susan makes me a scarf,
a fire to wind around
my neck,
a streak of sunset,
a tangerine tiger's tail,
a giant jaffa roll,
a finger of lava,

a neon sign
that tells the cold
to keep away.

Jenny Powell

The Bicycle

I have always been lucky.
When I was seven
my parents gave me
a red bicycle.

I rode it every day until
it became a part of me.

It had a basket on the front,
and my father attached a bell
to make doing the deliveries
more noticeable.

Pedalling up hills
pushed me so far inside my head
that only reaching the top
could bring me back out.

Going down, my mouth would open
as the world became flocks
of many-coloured birds
soaring into flight.

I loved that bicycle.

Lying in bed listening
to rain sheet against the window

and knowing that tomorrow
it was Monday,

I would get up and go
into the hall and stare at it,
consoled by the standing
of its beautiful silence.

James Brown

The Schoolbag

Coming home from school one day
My bag was noisy on the way,
I opened it and there I found
A barking, baying beagle hound.

I thought the howling wouldn't stop
But then a cat climbed in on top!

The beagle chased the cat about;
Fur went flying, claws came out,
I thought the yowling wouldn't stop
But then a chook flew in on top!

My schoolbag filled with feather fluff,
'O.K.,' I said, 'I've had enough!'

I thought the squawking wouldn't stop
But then a roo jumped in on top!
The kangaroo then bounced around
Kicking chicken, cat and hound.

I thought the fighting wouldn't stop
But then a band marched in on top!

'That's it!' I yelled above the din,
'Who gave you leave to walk right in?'

I grabbed my bag and shook it well
Dog, cat, bird, roo — out they fell,
Another shake and onto land
Crashed the big brass marching band.

Then home I went with increased pace,
My bag and rattling pencil case.

Fifi Colston

How to Swim a Length Under Water

(Recite in a single breath)

Pump up your lungs as far as they'll go
like a balloon that's just about to pop
do a long flat dive that rockets you
down the pool like a torpedo below
the surface grab armfuls of water
pushing it back past your hips so your
body shoots forward like a squid again
and again ready to burst again and
again straining to touch the wall again
and again and again and again until
you reach . . . THE END

Greg O'Connell

Night Swimming

I saw lights in the water
while I was swimming in the sea
one night.

They stuck onto my arms and legs.
Light streamed from the ends of my fingers and toes.
I flicked my feet like a fish
I drew circles with my hands
I shimmered like a star falling

in the deep dark water.

Kiri Piahana-Wong

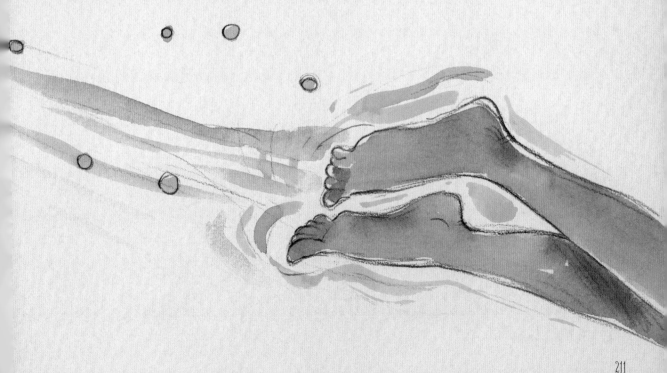

Colour Poem

Yellow is a peach
That drips on a shirt
Yellow are the spots
On my pretty new skirt.

Stella Baker, aged 9

The Same Old Mum

When Mum comes home from work,
the first thing she says is
'Put on the coffee, love.
I'll just go and change into something else.'
I put on the coffee and wait.

Will she change into a camel?
or a smiley green dragon?
or a chest of drawers?
or a triple-headed alien?
or maybe a super-mum
who cries 'Gazoo! Gazam!'

No, she always comes back as the same old Mum.
All she ever changes into
are her old home clothes.

Pauline Cartwright

The Sneeze

I'm going to sneeze.
Yes, I'm going to sneeze.
It's coming.
The sneeze is coming.
I can't stop it I can't stop it.

Ah . . . .
Ah . . . .

It's gone.
Nothing happened.
I didn't sneeze.
I know I won't sneeze now.

AH-TISHOOOOO!!!!!!!!!!!!

Roger Hall

The Dog-minding Machine

We have made a machine
For the busy dog owner:
It's a washer and walker
And thrower-of-boner;

With a brusher, comber,
A feeder, a patter,
A ball-throwing arm,
And a chaser-of-catter;

There's a cleaner of kennel
Complete with flea-catcher;
A cutter of meat
And a special back-scratcher;

A run-round-the-blocker
To make your dog fitter . . .
Won't you buy our machine?
It's the perfect Dog Sitter!

Joy Watson

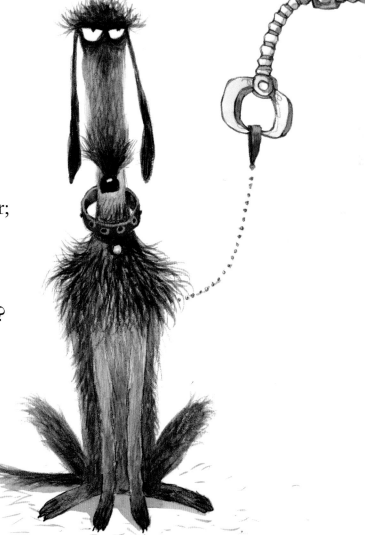

Don't Be Wet

(a poem for two voices)

So you think you're a fish, Mr —
Fin.
And your favourite game is —
Pool.
A film that you hated was —
Hook.
And you met all your friends in a —
School.

Your father's a piano —
Tuna.
So each morning you check on your —
Scales.
The best book you've read was called —
Jaws.
You're expert at telling such —
Tails.

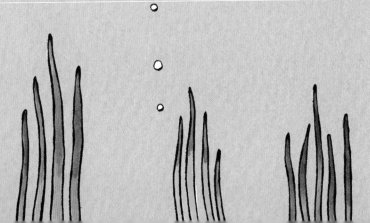

But you say there's a bully called —
Rod.
And he's trodden quite hard on your —
'Eel.
That made you yell out a loud —
Whale.
Mr Fin, you believe this?
It's reel!

David Hill

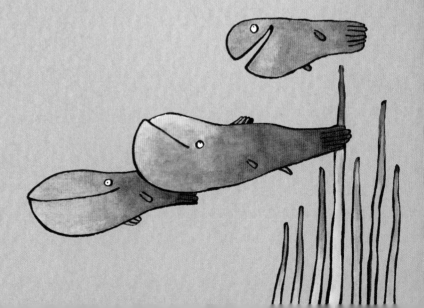

Injections

Our baby brother screams
When he gets his injections.
Nothing will stop him crying,
He's red as can be.

No waving bye bye,
No eating banana,
No biting Mum's phone,
No shaking the car key.

Nothing will stop him crying
Except cuddles.
Lots and lots of cuddles
From me.

Janice Marriott

A Grumpy Poem

Willy is down in the dumps.
His face has come up in bumps.
Every day it grows more hilly;
poor lumpy, bumpy, mumpy Willy.

Harry Ricketts

Packing My Bag for Mars

One ten-litre thermos flask
full of 240-volt electric eels
to charge my portable toaster
to toast my portable toast
and heat my potable cocoa

in case I get hungry.

One small bedroom-sized
gyroscope equipped with
hydraulic shock absorbers
and with stainless-steel
stabiliser fins on its bilge keel
in the event of a Mars-quake

in case I get alarmed.

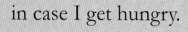

One pair of
large mohair-
merino wool mix
with possum fur
quadruple-knotted
triple-knitted
double-barrelled
argyle-patterned
work socks

in case I get cold.

One heavy-duty
extra-fleecy
multi-cellular
security blanket
with optional binocular
and piercing whistle
plus a satin-edged
silk-embroidered
thumb-hole

in case I get frightened.

One friend

in case I get lonely.

James Norcliffe

Tallest Cat

The tallest cat in the world went by
With his head stuck in the air.
The smallest cat in the world called out,
'Is there anyone home up there?'
The tallest cat in the world looked down,
Saw nobody in the street
And said to himself, 'Well, I'll be blowed!
I think I've got talking feet!'

Joy Cowley

Where the Mild Things Are!

Last night I heard the wind in the meadows
talking to the lion in the willows
about Captain Holeypants
and the Lord of the Rungs.
The wind said he had found
a chamber of sea crates,
a very hungry cat
the caterpillar in the hat
and Georgia's marbley medicine.
The lion said she had found
elastic Mr. Fox, an iron
an itch and a bathrobe,
and a series of fortunate events
over the pea and under bones.

Paula Green

The Puffin

Except for an occasional
Deep rumbling note
In its throat
A puffin
Says nuffin.

Shirley Gawith

Teeny-weeny Weta

Teeny-Weeny Weta climbed up the shiny flax,
down came the rain and washed poor Teeny back,
out came the sun and dried up all the rain,
then Teeny-Weeny Weta climbed up the flax again.

Peter Millett

Porridge

It's sludging, begrudging, not budging muck
With its rubbery, flubbery quick-sand suck.
It's silky, full milky — a popping swell
Has oatey, warm throaty, slight salty smell.

Churn it, turn it, careful — don't burn it!

Oh,
There's the slop, the soup and the droop of it
The grey and the splay and the scoop of it.
The sliming, the timing, the call of it
The sliding, the slipping, the fall of it.

Churn it, turn it, careful — don't burn it!

The scraping, the shaping, the peak of it
The oozing, the fizzing, the squeak of it
The trouble, the bubble, the catch of it
The grasping, the pull and the snatch of it.

Churn it, turn it, careful — don't burn it!

The mumble, the grumble, the slur of it
The heating, the beating, the stir of it.
The moulding, the folding, a bowl of it
The placing, the chasing, the search of it.

Churn it, turn it, careful — don't burn it!

The slickery, thickery paste of it
The pinning, the winning, the taste of it
The mud pool, the spoonful, the grasp of it
Then the hollow, the swallow, the last of it.

Churn it, turn it, careful — don't burn it!

The cooling, the pooling, the skin of it
The hosing, disposing, in bin of it
The rubbing, the scrubbing a lot of it
The cleaning, the gleaming, the pot of it!

Stephanie Mayne

The Sink

The sink is an ocean of bubbles
The sink is a lake full of foam
The sink is a beach lined with froth
The sink is a cloud far from home

The sink is a chest full of treasure
The sink is a reef packed with wrecks
The sink is a tub full of pleasure
The sink is in up to its neck

The sink has the warmth of a bath
The sink has a smell quite delicious
The sink has the soft pop of fizzy
I just wish the sink had no dishes.

Greg O'Connell

Spaghetti

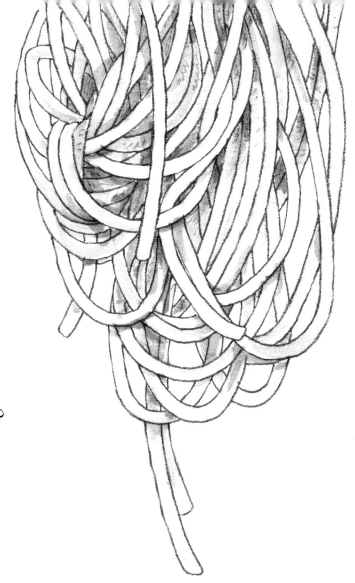

Spaghetti is loopy.
Spaghetti is droopy.
It's floppy
and ploppy
and sloppy
and gloppy.
It dribbles and dangles
and gets into tangles.

Is there more in the pot?
I like it a *lot*!

Pauline Cartwright

The Cat Who's Known as Flea

Once there was a little boy called Jeremiah Hay.
His father owned a dairy farm down Rotorua way.
His mother cooked and ironed, called family in for tea
While Jerry fed the chickens — and put down food for Flea.

Fleabag was a tabby, a large and fearsome cat
Who killed off all the mice, and frequently, a rat.
He prowled around the paddocks, roamed far and wide and free,
While Jerry caught the school bus — and left out food for Flea.

One day comes a letter from a nasty bank in town.
Dad has to sell his cattle and close the farm right down.
The family is heartbroken, but brave they try to be,
And Jerry packs his suitcase — including food for Flea.

They sell all their belongings, put Fleabag in a cage,
And move into the city, to a house that shows its age.
There is a little garden, with flowers and a tree
Where Jerry builds a tree hut — and is late with food for Flea.

When Mum installs some chickens, to lay their daily eggs,
Our Fleabag goes on licking at his tummy and his legs,
But Jerry has a birthday, and at his birthday tea
His present is hamster — no food that day for Flea.

And then it is some goldfish, a seagull and a duck,
The capture of a possum is thought a stroke of luck.

But when Dad brings a puppy home, the cat can plainly see
That Jerry has a new friend — and there's no place for Flea.

So Flea goes off exploring, down busy roads and lanes,
And finds himself just sitting, even when it rains,
Remembering his paddocks, the bed where he could be
Tucked into Jeremiah's knees — that's the place for Flea.

He grows thin and pale and cunning, as he has to search for food
In rubbish and in gardens, in angry bitter mood.
'What stupid, stupid people, trying hard to be
Farmers in the city! — Every animal but me!'

But then one day he hears, as he dreams a happy choice
Between chicken and fish fingers, an old familiar voice.
'Oh Flea, pusscat, where are you? Where are you, pusscat Flea?'
Is Jerry looking for him — to take him home to tea?

Then Jerry sees a tail, and then he sees a head,
'That's him!' cries Jeremiah, 'and I think that he is dead!'
But Fleabag lifts one eyelid and shakes his whiskers free.
He isn't quite forgotten — he's still their cat called Flea.

They take him home and feed him, again he's big and strong,
And he knows that they still love him — he'd got the story wrong.
There are lots of other pets around, but he will always be
Their Number One brave moggie — the cat who's known as Flea.

Tessa Duder

Little Furry Cats

Little furry cats
lick their paws
and carefully
sharpen their claws.

Little furry cats
will move like a flash
when someone
shuts a door with a crash.

Little furry cats
climb tall trees
and just love
to scratch your knees.

Little furry cats
are fond of long naps
in armchairs and seats
and adults' warm laps.

Little furry cats
will play the fool
with a pile of knitting
and a skein of wool.

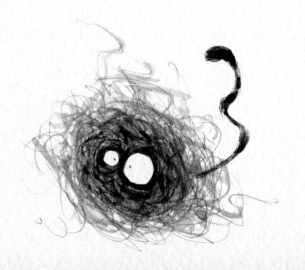

Little furry cats
sniff the gutter
the way they sniff
a lump of butter.

Little furry cats
slide on the roof
and generally act
awfully aloof.

Little furry cats
are nobody's fool;
they know what they know
without going to school.

Brian Turner

The Pumperknickle Pirate

Beware my purple pretty friend
for beneath your bed lays on end

A stinkent, stank, sorbed sod
that pokes and prods at your bod

Your toes he knows are what he likes
not injured mice and their bikes

Watch out, watch out
don't scream and shout

Beware my purple pretty friend
your feet are now near their end

He munches and crunches
on week old lunches

Spits and spatters
clicks and clatters

He will lay there — until he's fed
the Pumperknickle Pirate in your bed!

Sarah Aileen

The Snuggly Bed

One winter night when the snow lay deep
in my snuggly bed I went to sleep.
BUT! Just as I began to snore (Hrummmph!)
there came a KNOCK KNOCK KNOCKING at my door.

'Meow!' said the cat. 'My paws are froze.
I've got an icicle on my nose!
I'm cold from my tail to the top of my head.
Can I come and sleep in your snuggly bed?'

SO! I opened the door and the cat jumped in.

One winter night when the snow lay deep
the cat and me settled down to sleep.
BUT! Just as we began to snore (Hrummmph!)
there came a KNOCK KNOCK KNOCKING at my door.

'Woof!' said the dog. 'My paws are froze.
I've got an icicle on my nose!
I'm cold from my tail to the top of my head.
Can I come and sleep in your snuggly bed?'

SO! I opened the door and the dog jumped in.

One winter night when the snow lay deep
the cat and the dog and me settled down to sleep.
BUT! Just as we began to snore (Hrummmph!)
there was a KNOCK KNOCK KNOCKING at my door.

'Oink!' said the pig. 'My trotters are froze.
I've got an icicle on my nose.
I'm cold from my tail to the top of my head.
Can I sleep with you in your snuggly bed?'

SO! I opened the door and the pig jumped in.

One winter night when the snow lay deep
the cat and the dog and the pig and me settled down to sleep.
BUT! Just as we began to snore (Hrummmph!)
there came a KNOCK KNOCK KNOCKING at my door.

'Squeak!' said the mouse. 'My paws are froze.
I've got an icicle on my nose.
I'm cold from my tail to the top of my head.
Can I sleep with you in your snuggly bed?'

SO! I opened the door and the mouse jumped in.
Then I switched out the light.
'Nighty night!' I said.
'Now, let's all go to sleep
in the snuggly bed.'

BUT! The little mouse said
'I WANT TO SLEEP IN THE MIDDLE!'

And then the cat began to wriggle,
and the dog began to giggle
and the pig began to jiggle.
SO! I switched on the light.

'THAT'S ENOUGH!' I said.
'You've GOT to go to sleep in the snuggly bed!
You mustn't wriggle and giggle and fight!
Now, dream good dreams, and NIGHTY NIGHT.'

SO! That winter night
when the snow lay deep,
with the little mouse in the middle,
we
all
went
to
sleep.

Fiona Farrell

The Sound Collector

shhhh hh...

The sound collector,
he takes all the sound
you could make
in your small little house.
He is dressed in browns.
He takes all the sounds
and then he is off with a flash.
Although you will never see him
he will always come.
He will take sounds
like the bang of the frying pan
even the teacher's 'shhhhh!'
the sounds of kids talking,
the sounds he always finds.

Max Simpson, aged 7

Empty Hutch

Pepper's gone
she's left for good
I think she's found a neighbourhood
where dandelions fill the breeze
and carrots
grow as tall as trees

Elena de Roo

Winter

Everywhere the trees
are nevergreen.
The wind makes
my nose freeze.
The rain makes
a fast river
in our street.

There's a hole in the sky
where the rain falls out.
On the Desert Road
the storm
waterblasts our car.

At Whakapapa, the snow
is as white as a hospital room,
and as bright as the sun.
We slide down the mountain
on plastic bags.
Here we go.

Laura Ranger, written when she was 6

Pele

Pele picks feathers from the pavement
very carefully with his fingernails

even though mum says they're dirty
he knows treasure when he sees it.

The feathers flew through rainbows
he runs them under water

dries them in the hot sun
outside by the washing line.

At night he tells his ninjas about birds
how they create a memory of the land

the feathers fan out under his pillow
Pele falls asleep upon the sky.

Courtney Sina Meredith

Soft Leaf Falls of Light

Soft leaf falls of light
soft light falls of leaf
leaf soft light falls
light soft leaf falls
light falls leaf soft
light light light
soft leaf falls of light

Apirana Taylor

243

Fruits

With shaking fingers
grandad picks an apple for me
from his old backyard tree —
so juicy
so ripe
so sweet.

And as I eat
I see
that bent like a branch is grandad's back,
wrinkled like bark is his face,
furrowed like roots are his hands.

And I see
that I eat also the fruits of grandad —
his wise words,
his warm and loving ways —
apples given rich and ripe to me.

John Parker

When I Am Old and Wrinkled Like a Raisin

When I am old and wrinkled like a raisin
I will dance like a kite on the bucking back of the wind.
I won't look ahead at the few bright days I am facing
Or look back at the years trailing out like streamers behind.

Everyone else will be gone. The silence will seem to be mocking,
But I will dangle and dance in the bright and clear air of the day
Kicking my old stick legs in their red striped stockings.
An old leaf wrinkled and brown but golden and gay.

Dance, dance, little old feet. Spin on your halfpenny of time.
Roar, little old lion, in your meadow of cobwebs and rust
Till you burn with the fiery power of the dance and the rhyme
And fall back to the earth in a sprinkle of golden dust.

Margaret Mahy

245

Flight of the Penguins

Propelled by feathered wings —
flapping,
        swooping,
                gliding,
soaring on hidden currents,
skimming through clouded seas.
Penguins, flying in water.

Feana Tu'akoi

Swamp Kauri

The kauri logs
lay like dinosaurs
in the swamps
of the old world

Their black surfaces
like dragon's scales
hiding the golden
grain beneath

Jacqueline Crompton Ottaway

Peacocks

Peacocks can't run
As quickly as quails
And this is why peacocks
Have eyes in their tails.

Arthur Baysting

Chant of the Bats

One-winged? No — moving, moving.
Two-headed? No — moving, moving.
Three-lunged? No — moving, moving.
Four-stomached? No — moving, moving.
Five-legged? No — moving, moving.
Many there are of us all together,
swirling in a cloud of darkness,
so many you cannot separate us.
Our skins are as soft and sleek as leather.
We are bat beings — bats!
We frighten cats!
Leather rags spat from the mouth of a cave,
leather bags flying, wave upon wave.
We flap our wings from pockets and ledges,
flap flap flap from pozzies and perches —
we are radars and sonars,
squeakers and rustlers,
bumpers and bouncers and bickerers,
ultrasonic flick, flick, flickerers.
We float upwards into the night,
and land on trees
to screech and scratch —
black, black, black!
Slowly we flap, a crowd of bats.
We are bat beings, bat creatures —
bats, bats, bats!

David Eggleton

Caterpillar

(inspired by the children's game in Cantonese)

Touch,
touch the little worm.
Watch it writhe
and watch it squirm.
Watch it spinning
round and down.
Watch it as it
spins a gown.
Wait a while —
it's made a house!
A house in green
all strung with lights
in golden threads
and beads of jade.
A tiny window
winks and glows.
You watch and wait
and hope and hope.
Slow, slow
the day arrives.
Look through the pane,
there's someone new.
Watch them as they
nudge and pry.

They push and push
they try and try.
The window opens
they slide right through.
They dry their wings —
then fly, fly, FLY!

Renee Liang

Elk

An elk, I think,
is loosely a moose:
but I'm not quite sure
if my first idea
is mostly fictionary
so soon I'm up off my chair
and into the dictionary
which tells me
in a quiet kind of clear
that an elk in fact
is a large sort of deer.

Elk, elk: when you say it aloud
it has a slow sloping sound
with a soft kind of swallow,
as if elk hips sway and flow
like hot milk and melted marshmallow —

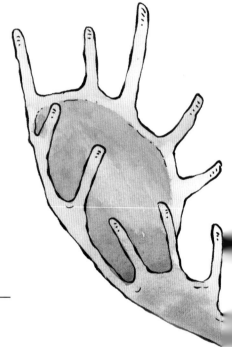

but this elk is all talk, type,
ink and screen-light:
I think if a live elk
loomed up to press the boot
of its grassy breath
against my neck
I'd be too spooked by its bulk
to even squeak an *eek*;
all sappy notions of milky melt flattened

by the crashing chandelier of its antlers
and the dung-pong cannonball
of its mossy, moosey hoof . . .

(For, yes, a moose, I see now from the dictionary,
is also a cousin from the deer family:
gallop-de-loop,
we're back at the start:
to say an elk's of moose ilk
will pass!)

Emma Neale

The Song of the Kingfisher

Why do you sit, so dreamily dreamily,
Kingfisher over the stream
Silent your beak, and silent the water,
What is your dream?

A falling, a flashing of blue and of silver,
Child, he is deep in the stream,
Prey in his beak and fear in the water
That was his dream!

Eileen Duggan

Tūī

Tūī, tūī
scrapes and squawks

drags sounds
from a box

checking out the different noises
that can work as tūī voices.

Mary Cresswell

Morning on the Marae

Morning on the marae
wakes warm-pillowed,
sleepy-eyed.

Morning on the marae
yawns foggy-breathed,
wide-stretched.

'Tihe mauri ora!'

Room 7 sleepover
stacks mattresses,
rolls sleeping bags.

Room 7 sleepover
smells bacon sizzling,
toast popping,

Tangata whenua
hear puku rumbling,
lips smacking.

'Haere mai ki te kai!'

It's breakfast time
on the marae.

Sue Gibbison

Skipping

thack thack rope line
cuts the air and thacks the ground
makes a space
an egg to jump in
jump thack jump thack
OW!
I'm out
turning the rope line
arm round and round
my friend jumps in and
jump thack jump thack

we could leap the world and fly
springs in our knees
and our eyes full of sky

Raewyn Alexander

Clocks

Clocks
are very clever things
with numbers
   pendulums
     and springs.
Wound up
they quietly tick away,
unnoticed,
all throughout the day
but
if you wake,
   curled warm
     and tight
during the long dark
of the night,
it's strange
   that even
     little clocks
can fill the house
with loud
   TICK
     TOCKS.

Peggy Dunstan

tick
tock
tick
tock
tick
tock
tick
tock
tick
tock
tick

Dennis Made a Soccer Ball

Starting small,
Dennis made a soccer ball.

Paper layers crunched together,
soon the soccer ball grew bigger.

Dennis played it down the street,
dashing moves with dancing feet.

He passed it to his friends who came,
they turned the dance into a game.

Kicked by all the local players,
the soccer ball soon lost some layers.

Feint and cross, shoot and score,
the ball diminished even more.

Too small to stay a soccer ball . . .
Said Dennis, 'Let's play tennis.'

Bill Nagelkerke

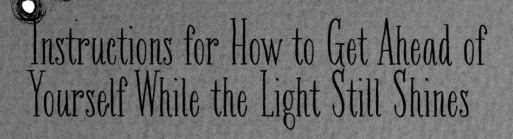

Instructions for How to Get Ahead of Yourself While the Light Still Shines

If you have a bike, get on it at night
and go to the top of the Brooklyn hill.

When you reach the top
start smiling — this is Happy Valley Road.

Pedal at first, then let the road take you down
into the dark as black as underground
broken by circles of yellow lowered by the street
lights.

As you come to each light
you will notice a figure
racing up behind.
Don't be scared
this is you creeping up on yourself.
As you pass under the light
you will sail past yourself into the night.

Jenny Bornholdt

Ghost Bride

Want to end up wide-eyed?
Feeling like your stomach died?
Presented with the greatest pride
Welcome to our wildest ride

Like it on the chilly side?
Smile so wide, it's freeze-dried?
Keep that seat-belt firmly tied
Disembarking now denied!

Just a little terrified?
Perhaps a tiny tongue-tied?
Wait until you meet your guide
You'll wish you never took *this* ride

Teeth, as green as snake's hide
Blood of pure formaldehyde
She'll turn your marrow cold inside
Say hello to
      Ghost Bride!

Elena de Roo

Midnight Motorway

In between
Huge roller machines
The sealing team
Works the night.
Like cats,
Their eyes gleam:
Orange lights
Through bitumen
Steam.

Alan Bagnall

Window Cleaners

There they were this morning,
High up on an office block.

One was polishing the sun,
Another rinsing fleecy clouds,
A third rubbing the blue sky.

If I come back tonight,
Will they still be there —

One scrubbing the shooting stars,
Another washing the moon,
A third wiping down the Milky Way?

David Hill

After-shocks

now there are cracks in the bathroom
it makes sense to welcome
strangers from an unstable world

behind the taps
an orange spider treads water

and out of this daring
occupies a new position

one flick of my finger
and the spider would disappear

let it rest on the basin curve

Jan Hutchison

Gumboot Weather

When we can't hear the telly, it's raining so hard
we grab Mum's umbrella and run for the yard
then together, we giggle, my brother and I
in our drumming, umbrella hut under the sky

Elena de Roo

Ecology

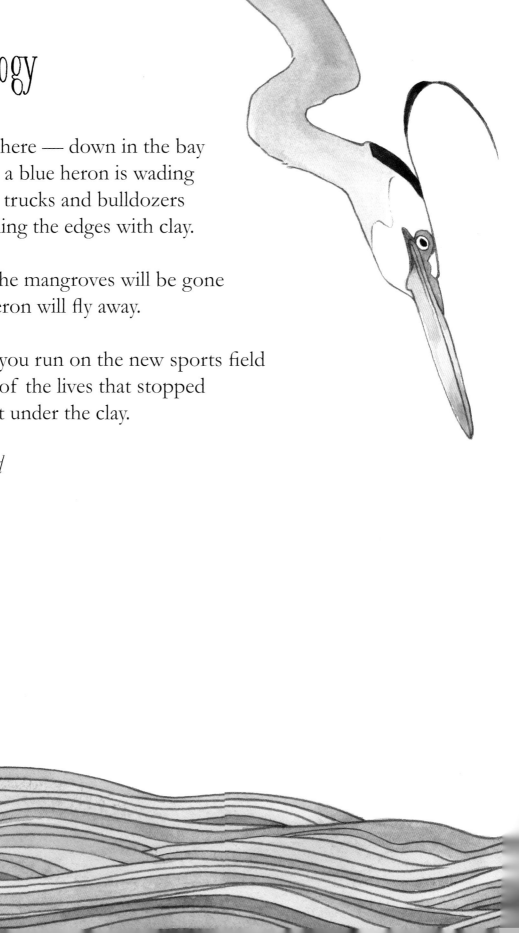

Look there — down in the bay
Where a blue heron is wading
Dump trucks and bulldozers
Are filling the edges with clay.

Soon the mangroves will be gone
The heron will fly away.

When you run on the new sports field
Think of the lives that stopped
Six feet under the clay.

C K Stead

The Sea

I think I'll go and look at the sea
curled up in the bay.
Sometimes, when the tide is out,
it tries to sneak away.

There it is! It's come up close
to lap the shore like a cat
with a sparkle on its bright blue fur
and the sun warming its back.

Listen, and you'll hear it purr
as it snuggles up to the land.
Yesterday, in the wind and rain,
it dug huge holes in the sand.

It hurled great boulders on the beach
and piled-up driftwood stacks.
It leapt over the harbour wall
and turned boats on their backs.

Today it hardly moves at all.
Sun-stroked, it barely breathes.
Small breezes stir its hidden depths
as it rests but never sleeps.

Peter Bland

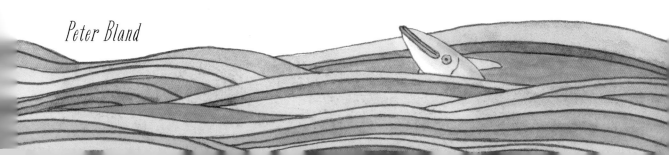

Poem for Anzac Day

Anzac poppy,
small and sweet,

crushed beneath the soldiers' feet.

Fragile petals,
red as blood,

spilled upon the Flanders mud.

Judy Raymond

My Grandad's Hands

My grandad's hands
are leathery nailbags;
his back, a straight ladder;
his legs, solid posts.
His laugh is a lost hammer;
his breath, sawdust in the wind.
Lying
peaceful as silence,
my grandad
is wrapped in wood.

Greg O'Connell

Sowing Seeds with Milly

There's the bee
& the birds down from the trees
beaking in the lawn

here we go with our hands
I say to the small yellow dress
growing beside me

the cricket bat lying face down
is waiting
for Jack's hands to wake

now in goes the seed
in it goes

& when I am not here to remember to water
you will be

Richard Langston

Milly, 8, Contemplates Homework

Under sun-streaked strands of hair
looped above
the pink of her mind

In yellow dressing-gown
& wiggling feet

she touches her nose,
with a pondering finger
and says,

Dad,
is it time
for bed yet?

Richard Langston

I Know Just About Everything Now That I Know About . . .

Rings of trees, butterfly wings.
Insects that turn each other into slaves.
How many times it is possible to fold
a single sheet of paper.
Black holes. Red dwarfs.
Watching an eclipse
through a pinhole in cardboard.
Fixing bicycle tyres with old spoons
and a bucket of water.
Why you must never touch
the sticky yellow stamen
of an arum lily.
Pouches on wallabies and kangaroos.
Tectonic plates. Continental drift.
Simple fractions. Complex numbers.
And that really weird thing about sea horses.

Maria McMillan

Hush! Hush! Hush!

'Hush! Hush! Hush!' sings the wind on the hill.
'Hush, you rackety world. Hold still!'
The ocean sings as it strokes the land.
'Shush!' sigh the waves on the soft, sea sand.
'Hush!' says the moon looking out of the night.
'Hush to my darling, my heart's delight.'

Margaret Mahy

Owl

Night owl
      White owl
Cold stars
      Moon red

Attic light
      Fire bright
Earth sleep
      Warm bed

Peter Bland

Waxing and Waning

Your face of silver
lights the sky
a perfect plate
of pale moon pie

and if I took
a bite of you
then I'd be full
and you'd be new

Elena de Roo

275

The Old Owl

'Tu whit! Tu whoo!'
The old owl said —
'Pack your toys
And get ready for bed.

'As I sit on the branch
Of a grey gum tree
There's nobody here
But the moon and me;

'There's nobody here
But me and the moon,
And I'll go a-hunting
For my supper soon.

'A beetle, a bug
And a brown field mouse,
I'll bring them home
To my gum tree house.

'I'm old as old,
And wise as wise,
And I see in the dark
With my great round eyes.

'So hurry and scurry,'
The old owl said —
'Pack your toys
And get ready for bed.'

James K Baxter

A Lullaby

Here is the world in which you sing.
Here is your sleepy cry.
Here is your sleepy father.
And here the sleepy sky.

Here is the sleepy mountain,
and here the sleepy sea.
Here is your sleepy mother.
Sleep safe with me.

Here is pohutukawa,
here is the magpie's eye,
here is the wind in branches
going by.

Here is a heart to beat with yours,
here is your windy smile.
Here are these arms to hold you
for a while.

Here is the world in which you sleep,
and here the sleepy sea.
Here is your sleepy mother.
Sleep safe with me.

Bill Manhire

Haere Mai ki te Moe

Hear old weka crying,
kee-ark, kee-ark, kee-ark.
Hear the night wind sighing,
hear the farm dogs bark.
Tamariki, tamariki,
haere mai ki te moe.

Hear the call of ruru,
morepork, morepork, morepork.
Hear flying beetle huhu,
hear the pine trees talk.
Tamariki, tamariki,
haere mai ki te moe.

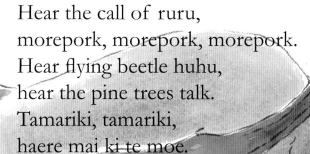

Papatūānuku
calls a thousand ways,
to sleepy tamariki
at the end of busy days.
Tamariki, tamariki,
haere mai ki te moe.

Listen to the waiata
of gentle Mother Earth,
rest in the aroha
of she who gave you birth.
Tamariki, tamariki,
haere mai ki te moe.

Joy Cowley

Acknowledgements

Grateful acknowledgement is made to the following poets and copyright holders for permission to reproduce these poems. Every effort has been made to contact the copyright holders. If you have further information, please contact the publisher.

Sarah Aileen, 'Birthday Cake Recipe', 'The Pumperknickle Pirate,' unpublished

Raewyn Alexander, 'Skipping' in *The School Journal*, 1996, 3:1 (Ministry of Education)

Alan Bagnall, 'Midnight Motorway' in *The School Journal*, 1998, 3:2 (Ministry of Education); 'My Cat' in *100 New Zealand Poems for Children* (Random House, 1999)

James K Baxter, 'Little Mr Mushroom', 'Spring-heeled Jack', 'The Big Black Whale', 'The Growly Bear', 'The Old Owl', 'The Ships' in *The Tree House and Other Poems for Children* (Price Milburn, 1974). Permission courtesy of the James K Baxter Trust

Arthur Baysting, 'Peacocks' in *Another 100 Poems for Children* (Random House, 2001)

Gavin Bishop, 'Raisin' Chickens', unpublished

Peter Bland, 'Our Dog Charlie', 'Owl', 'Rhymes', 'The Bed Boat', 'The Night Kite' in *The Night Kite* (Mallinson Rendel, 2004); 'Sunflowers', 'The Sea' in *When Gulls Fly High* (Puffin, 2011)

Jenny Bornholdt, 'Giddy' in *These Days* (Victoria University Press, 2000); 'Instructions for How to Get Ahead of Yourself While the Light Still Shines' in *The School Journal*, 2003, 4:3 (Ministry of Education)

Sarah Broom, 'Ode to the Orange', unpublished. Permission courtesy of Michael Gleissner

James Brown, 'The Bicycle' in *The Year of the Bicycle* (Victoria University Press, 2006)

Rachel Bush, 'Early' in *The School Journal*, 2011, 3:1 (Ministry of Education)

Alistair Te Ariki Campbell, 'Haiku' in *Blue Rain* (Wai-te-ata Press, 1967)

Pauline Cartwright, 'From the Hill' in *The School Journal*, 1994, 3:3; 'The Same Old Mum' in *100 New Zealand Poems for Children* (Random House, 1999); 'Spaghetti' in *The School Journal*, 2001, 1:4 (Ministry of Education)

Wendy Clarke, 'Shearing Shed' in *The School Journal*, May 2012, Level 2 (Ministry of Education)

Glenn Colquhoun, 'In Other Words' in *An Explanation of Poetry to My Father* (Steele Roberts, 2001)

Fifi Colston, 'The Schoolbag', unpublished

Joy Cowley, 'My Cat', 'Tallest Cat', 'Tree Cat' in *Pawprints in the Butter: A Collection of Cat Poems* (Mallinson Rendel, 1991); 'Elephap Rap', 'The Bookshop Elephant' in *Elephant Rhymes* (Scholastic, 1997); 'Haere Mai ki te Moe' in *A Book of Pacific Lullabies*, ed. Tessa Duder (HarperCollins, 2001)

Mary Cresswell, 'Tūī' in *The School Journal*, 2000, 3:3 (Ministry of Education)

Jacqueline Crompton Ottaway, 'Swamp Kauri', unpublished

Ruth Dallas, 'A Fly' in *Shadow Show* (Caxton Press, 1968); 'Rain on the Roof' in *The School Journal*, 1987, 1:4 (Ministry of Education)

Elena de Roo, 'Snorkelling' in *The School Magazine Countdown*, 2007, 92:7; 'Waxing and Waning' in *The School Magazine Countdown*, 2008, 93:2 (NSW Dept Education); 'Empty Hutch', 'Ghost Bride', 'Gumboot Weather', 'My Kind of Day', 'Words', unpublished

Melanie Drewery, 'If Stars Were Stitches', 'Out in the Night Time' in *Stories from Our Night Sky* (Puffin, 2009)

Doc Drumheller, 'Orowaiti Road', unpublished

Tessa Duder, 'The Cat Who's Known as Flea', in *The Great New Zealand Activity Book*, ed. Fifi Colston (New Zealand Illustrators Guild, 2000)

Eileen Duggan, 'The Song of the Kingfisher' in *New Zealand Bird Songs* (Harry H Tombs, 1929)

Peggy Dunstan, 'Bits and Pieces', 'Driving Through the Apple Orchards' in *In and Out the Windows: Poems for Children* (Hodder & Stoughton, 1979); 'Clocks' in *Behind the Stars: Poems for Children* (Hodder & Stoughton, 1986); 'Night Countdown' in *The School Journal*, 1992, 2:2 (Ministry of Education); 'Joshua Jones' in *The Puffin Treasury of New Zealand Children's Stories*, ed. Jenni Keestra (Puffin, 2005)

Lauris Edmond, 'Sea Creatures', 'Tuatara' in *Another 100 New Zealand Poems for Children* (Random House, 2001). Permission courtesy of the Estate of Lauris Edmond

David Eggleton, 'Chant of the Bats', unpublished

Fiona Farrell, 'The Vagabond Tomato' in *The School Journal*, 1993, 2:4 (Ministry of Education); 'Once a Little Kiwifruit' in *Another 100 New Zealand Poems for Children* (Random House, 2001); 'Shiny', 'The Snuggly Bed', unpublished

Tamsin Flynn, 'Old Man Wind', unpublished

Janet Frame, 'The Cat of Habit', 'The Old Bull' in *The Goose Bath* (Vintage, 2006). Permission courtesy of the Janet Frame Estate

Bernard Gadd, 'The Fantail Requests' in *100 New Zealand Poems for Children* (Random House, 1999)

Jon Gadsby, 'Goldfish', 'Hippopotamus', 'Scaly Tail the Rat' in *A Book of Beasts* (Hodder & Stoughton, 1984)

Shirley Gawith, 'Mr Nelligan's Nightshirt', 'Scratchy Cats' in *Mr Nelligan's Nightshirt: Cat Poems* (D'Urville Press, 1991); 'The Armadillo', 'The Puffin' in *Time for a Rhyme* (TreeHouse, 1995)

Sue Gibbison, 'Morning on the Marae' in *The School Journal*, 2007, 1:1 (Ministry of Education)

Denis Glover, 'Threnody' in *The Wind and the Sand* (Caxton Press, 1945); 'The Gentle Rain' in *Enter Without Knocking* (Pegasus Press, 1964). Permission courtesy of the Denis Glover Estate

Patricia Grace, 'Whisper to Me' in *A Book of Pacific Lullabies*, ed. Tessa Duder (HarperCollins, 2001)

Paula Green, 'An Elephanty Poem', 'The Bonnet Macaque: An Omnivore' in *Flamingo Bendalingo* (Auckland University Press, 2006); 'The Albadile and the Crocotross', 'Where the Mild Things Are!' in *Macaroni Moon* (Random House, 2009); 'The Tūī' in *The Letterbox Cat and Other Poems* (Scholastic, 2014)

Claire Gummer, 'And What Are These?', 'Who Am I?', unpublished

Roger Hall, 'The Sneeze' in *Another 100 New Zealand Poems for Children* (Random House, 2001)

Siobhan Harvey, 'Cloud' in *JAAM*, 31 September 2013

Dinah Hawken, 'Earth' in *Water, Leaves, Stones* (Victoria University Press, 1995)

David Hill, 'Don't Be Wet' in *The School Journal*, 1994, 3:3; 'Window Cleaners' in *The School Journal*, 2002, 4:1; 'Seasons' in *The School Journal*, 2005, 2:4 (Ministry of Education)

Terrie Huege de Serville, 'Storm' in *The School Journal*, 2004, 1:4 (Ministry of Education)

Sam Hunt, 'We Could Just Disappear', 'Four Bow-wow Poems' in *South into Winter* (Alister Taylor, 1973); 'Christmas 1953' in *Knucklebones: Poems 1962–2012* (Craig Potton, 2012)

Jan Hutchison, 'After-shocks' in *The Press*, 2012

Anna Jackson, 'A Swan Plant in the Kitchen' in *The School Journal*, 2006, 4:2 (Ministry of Education); 'Ice Trolls', 'Pekapeka', 'Tuatara', unpublished

Helen Jacobs, 'Monsters', unpublished

Adrienne Jansen, 'The Wind Is Tired of Being Blamed for Everything' in *4th Floor Literary Journal* (Whitireia Publishing, 2011); 'Winter Fly', unpublished

Gwenyth Jones, 'Skipping Rhyme' in *100 New Zealand Poems for Children* (Random House, 1999); 'Ups a Daisy' in *The School Journal*, 1994, 1:3 (Ministry of Education)

Vivienne Joseph, 'Palomino' in *100 New Zealand Poems for Children* (Random House, 1999)

Phil Kawana, 'Whanganui-a-tara' in *Doors: A Contemporary New Zealand Poetry Selection*, ed. Terry Locke (Leaders Press, 2000)

Bev Kemp, 'Washday for the Clouds' in *100 New Zealand Poems for Children* (Random House, 1999)

Richard Langston, 'Sowing Seeds with Milly' in *Henry, Come See the Blue* (Fitzbeck Publishing, 2005); 'Milly, 8, Contemplates Homework', 'The Sapling Tree', unpublished

Michele Leggott, 'Where's the Winter Wren' in *Milk & Honey* (Auckland University Press, 2005)

Renee Liang, 'Caterpillar', unpublished

Margaret Mahy, 'If You Feel Blue, Get on Your Ski-doo' in *Another 100 Poems for Children* (Random House, 2001); 'George's Pet', 'My Sister', 'The Dictionary Bird', 'The Reluctant Hero, or Barefoot in the Snow' in *Nonstop Nonsense* (JM Dent & Sons, 1977); 'Further Adventures of Humpty Dumpty', 'Hush! Hush! Hush!', 'When I Am Old and Wrinkled Like a Raisin' in *The Word Witch* (HarperCollins, 2009)

John Malone, 'Big Blue Mouth' in *The School Journal*, 2007, 1:5; 'The Red Pencil Sharpener' in *The School Journal*, February 2012, Level 2 (Ministry of Education)

Bill Manhire, 'It Is Nearly Summer' in *How to Take Your Clothes Off at the Picnic* (Wai-te-ata

Press, 1977); 'Red Horse' in *Good Looks* (Auckland University Press, 1982); 'Girl Reading' in *Zoetropes* (Allen & Unwin, 1984); 'A Lullaby', 'The Lid Slides Back' in *Victims of Lightning* (Victoria University Press, 2010)

Katherine Mansfield, 'Out in the Garden' in *The Candle Fairy* (Alister Taylor, 1991)

Janice Marriott, 'Injections', 'It's More Simple for Dogs', 'Weather Forecast', unpublished

Stephanie Mayne, 'Jellyfish', 'Porridge', 'Zoo Chimpanzee', unpublished

Rachel McAlpine, 'Skin-diving' in *100 New Zealand Poems for Children* (Random House, 1999); 'Computers Can't Scoot' in *Another 100 New Zealand Poems for Children* (Random House, 2001)

Anne McDonell, 'Christmas Festival' in *The School Journal*, 1991, 2:1 (Ministry of Education)

Maria McMillan, 'I Know Just About Everything Now That I Know About …' in *The School Journal*, 2007, 4:1 (Ministry of Education)

Cilla McQueen, 'Dogwobble' in *Benzina* (John McIndoe, 1988)

Courtney Sina Meredith, 'Pele', unpublished

Kyle Mewburn, 'Rainy Day Washaway', unpublished

Peter Millet, 'Mary, Mary', 'Teeny-weeny Weta' in *Humpty Rugby and Other Classic Kiwi Rhymes* (Penguin, 2008)

Nadia Moon, 'Pāua' in *The School Journal*, 2005, 1:3 (Ministry of Education)

Bill Nagelkerke, 'Rain' in *Another 100 New Zealand Poems for Children* (Random House, 2001); 'At Night', 'A Visit to the Beachside Library', 'Bottled Stars', 'Dennis Made a Soccer Ball', unpublished

Emma Neale, 'Elk', unpublished

James Norcliffe, 'Packing My Bag for Mars' in *Packing My Bag for Mars* (Clerestory Press, 2012); 'First You Get the Knives and Forks', unpublished

Greg O'Connell, 'The Sink' in *The School Journal*, 2008, 3:3; 'Kick-off' in *The School Journal*, 2011, 2:2; 'How to Swim a Length Under Water' in *The School Journal*, October 2011, Level 2; 'My Grandad's Hands' in *The School Journal*, November 2011, Level 3 (Ministry of Education); 'What My Dragon Likes', unpublished

John Parker, 'Fried, Please' in *The School Journal*, 1986, 2:3; 'Mr Swash' in *The School Journal*, 1993, 1:4; 'The Bumble-bee Postie' in *The School Journal*, 1996, 1:2; 'Cocoon' in *The School Journal*, 2002, 1:4 (Ministry of Education); 'Jet-whales' in *Another 100 New Zealand Poems for Children* (Random House, 2001); 'Finding a Poem', 'Fruits', unpublished

Ruth Paul, 'Sparkle', unpublished

Kiri Piahana-Wong, 'Night Swimming' in *Night Swimming* (Anahera Press, 2013)

Jenny Powell, 'The Scarf' in *The School Journal*, 2004, 3:1; 'Fake Blood' in *The School Journal*, 2005, 3:3 (Ministry of Education)

Elizabeth Pulford, 'Sun Sonata' in *The School Journal*, 2010, 3:2 (Ministry of Education)

Laura Ranger, 'Autumn Leaves', 'Mum', 'The Alien', 'Tulip Sunday', 'Winter' in *Laura's Poems* (Godwit, 1995)

Gloria Rawlinson, 'Soapsuds' in *Gloria's Book* (Whitcombe & Tombs, 1932)

Judy Raymond, 'Poem for Anzac Day' in *The School Journal*, February 2012, Level 2 (Ministry of Education)

Harry Ricketts, 'A Grumpy Poem' in *Coming Under Scrutiny* (cultural and political booklet, 1989)

Elizabeth Smither, 'The Daisy' in *I'm Glad the Sky is Painted Blue*, ed. Rosalyn Barnett (Mallinson Rendel, 1993); 'Big Birds and Small' in *The School Journal*, 1994, 2:2 (Ministry of Education)

C K Stead, 'Ecology', 'Just for the Record' in *Quesada: Poems 1972–1974* (The Shed, 1975)

Robert Sullivan, 'Bright 1' in *Star Waka* (Auckland University Press, 1999)

Melinda Szymanik, 'Fancy', unpublished

Apirana Taylor, 'Haka', 'Huri Huri' in *Te Ata Kura: The Red-tipped Dawn* (Canterbury University Press, 2004); 'Leap Frog' in *Eyes of the Ruru* (Voice Press, 1979); 'Soft Leaf Falls of Light', 'Thunder God' in *Soft Leaf Falls of the Moon* (Pohutukawa Press, 1996)

Louise Tomlinson, 'Nanny' in *The School Journal*, 1997, 3:1 (Ministry of Education)

Feana Tu'akoi, 'Spiders' in *Another 100 New Zealand Poems for Children* (Random House, 2001); 'Kai 'Umu' in *The School Journal*, 2002, 1:1; 'Flight of the Penguins' in *The School Journal*, 2012, 1:2 (Ministry of Education)

Brian Turner, 'Little Furry Cats' in *The School Journal*, 1995, 1:5; 'Bumbles' in *The School Journal*, 2005, 1:1 (Ministry of Education)

Hone Tuwhare, 'Haiku 1', 'Rain' in *Come Rain Hail* (The Bibliography Room, University of Otago, 1970); 'Children's Tale' in *Making a Fist of It* (Jackstraw Press, 1978)

S K Vickery, 'Windscreen Wiper' in *Another 100 New Zealand Poems for Children* (Random House, 2001)

Joy Watson, 'The Dog-minding Machine' in *Something Zany: A Miscellany*, ed. Gwen Gawith (Scholastic, 1992); 'The Elephant Bird' in *Worms Squirm . . . And Other Poems* (Scholastic, 2007)

Albert Wendt, 'Garden 5' in *From Mānoa to a Ponsonby Garden* (Auckland University Press, 2012)

Belinda Wong, 'A Chinese Song' in *The School Journal*, 2007, 3:1 (Ministry of Education)

Sue Wootton, 'Jimbo' in *The School Journal*, 2011, 2:1; 'The Second-hand Tent' in *The School Journal*, 2008, 2:2 (Ministry of Education); 'The Braid of Rivers', 'Wet Spell', unpublished

Ashleigh Young, 'Wild Ideas' in *The School Journal*, 2009, 4:3 (Ministry of Education)

Thanks

Special thanks to:

Skye Atkins, Redcliffs School, Christchurch

Charlie Aubrey, Freemans Bay School, Auckland

Stella Baker, Arapohue Primary School, Dargaville

Lachlan Boniface, Remarkables Primary School, Queenstown

Emily Boulton, Maihiihi Primary School, Otorohanga

Henry Eglinton, Medbury School, Christchurch

Anne-Marie Groves, Gladstone Primary School, Auckland

Holly Guthrie, St Canice's School, Westport, via The School for
    Young Writers, Christchurch

Nathan Hodge, St Brigid's School, Wellington

Amanda MacDonald-Keepa, St Mary's Catholic School, Otorohanga

Eden Matthews, Gladstone Primary School, Auckland

Sofia Pawley, Ellerslie Primary School, Auckland

Becky Reid, Arrowtown School

Adam Scammell, East Taieri School, Dunedin

Max Simpson, Remarkables Primary School, Queenstown

Caleb Stewart, Russley School, Christchurch

Alexandra Swain, Freeville Primary School, Christchurch, via The
    School for Young Writers, Christchurch

Mac van den Heuvel, St Brigid's School, Wellington

Luke Walker, Manurewa East Primary School, Auckland

Madeleine Williams, Newbury School, Palmerston North

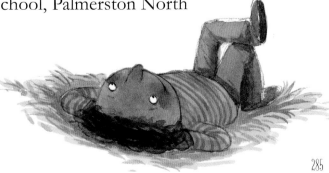

Index

Jenny Cooper has illustrated more than 70 books, working full-time as a freelance illustrator for the last 20 years. She has been nominated for the LIANZA Russell Clark Illustration Award twice, and awarded the Storylines Notable Book Award six times. She was the 2015 recipient of the Arts Foundation Mallinson Rendel Illustrators Award. In 2015 she also won the Picture Book category of the New Zealand Book Awards, for *Jim's Letters*. She specialises in illustrating in a realistic style for Pacific Island and Maori children, as well as books for younger readers.

Jenny has continuing ties with her husband's family in Western Samoa. She works from home, and raised her two children entirely from the proceeds of her illustration. After the Christchurch earthquakes, she moved with her partner, Chris, to Amberley in North Canterbury, where she battles the nor'wester and nurses an acre of young trees.